WHILE YOU WERE SWEEPING

A Riley Thomas Novella

By Christy Barritt

CHRISTY BARRITT

While You Were Sweeping: A Novella
Copyright 2015 by Christy Barritt

Published by River Heights Press

Cover design by The Killion Group

The persons and events portrayed in this work are the creation of the author, and any resemblance to persons living or dead is purely coincidental.

Other Books by Christy Barritt

Squeaky Clean Mysteries:
#1 Hazardous Duty
#2 Suspicious Minds
#2.5 It Came Upon a Midnight Crime
#3 Organized Grime
#4 Dirty Deeds
#5 The Scum of All Fears
#6 To Love, Honor, and Perish
#7 Mucky Streak
#8 Foul Play
#9 Broom and Gloom
#10 Dust and Obey (coming in 2015)

The Sierra Files
#1 Pounced
#2 Hunted
#2.5 Pranced (a Christmas novella)
#3 Rattled (coming in 2015)

The Gabby St. Claire Diaries (a tween mystery series)
#1 The Curtain Call Caper
#2 The Disappearing Dog Dilemma
#3 The Bungled Bike Burglaries

Holly Anna Paladin Mysteries
#1 Random Acts of Murder
#2 Random Acts of Malice (coming in 2015)

Carolina Moon series
#1 Home Before Dark
#2 Gone by Dark (coming in 2015)

Suburban Sleuth Mysteries:
#1 Death of the Couch Potato's Wife

Romantic Suspense:
Keeping Guard
The Last Target
Race Against Time
Ricochet
Key Witness
Lifeline
High-Stakes Holiday Reunion
Desperate Measures
Hidden Agenda (coming in March 2015)

Romantic Mystery:
The Good Girl

Suspense:
The Trouble with Perfect
Dubiosity

Nonfiction:
Changed: True Stories of Finding God through Christian Music
The Novel in Me: The Beginner's Guide to Writing and Publishing a Novel

A special thank you to all my Squeaky Clean readers who've lived this series with me. I hope you enjoy this story from Riley's perspective. I can't wait to see what the future holds!

Note: For those following the Squeaky Clean series, this book takes place between *Mucky Streak* and *Foul Play*.

CHRISTY BARRITT

CHAPTER 1

Riley Thomas stared at the phone in his hands, re-reading the message he'd typed there. As his finger hovered over the SEND button, his heart lurched at the impact of each word.

He squeezed his eyes shut.

What he'd written was raw and honest. He'd poured out his heart in those words.

Which meant he probably shouldn't let this note go any farther.

With a weight pressing on his shoulders, he finally wedged his eyes open and hit DELETE. He couldn't let himself be this truthful. It was in *his* own best interest to have this conversation, but he'd turn the life of the person receiving it upside down. He needed to get that through his thick skull.

He stood from the bench overlooking the lake behind his parents' house and shoved the phone into the back pocket of his jeans. With tension still tight across his shoulders, he jammed his hands into the pockets of his leather coat to ward away the nippy air. The wind was brisk and unseasonably chilly thanks to a cold snap in the area.

With one more melancholy sigh, he began trudging back toward his parents' place. It had been a long day, filled with grueling therapy and a dependence on his loved ones that he'd prefer not be there, especially at his age. It was just after five o'clock, and the sun was already setting, casting orange hues across the lake that made everything seem warmer than it actually was.

As he stepped around a bend of trees, a sound cracked through the air.

Riley instinctively ducked behind a tree, his heart stammering out of control.

Was that a . . . gunshot?

Something tried to flash into his mind: images, memories that were long forgotten and buried. They lingered beneath the surface, fighting against his other thoughts, against his survival instincts, clawing their way from the deep recesses of his brain and trying to emerge. He leaned against the tree, trying to keep his balance as his head swam with repressed memories.

Was his mind playing tricks on him? Or had that actually been the sound of a gun discharging?

Get a grip, Riley. Think. Calm down.

He sucked in a deep breath, trying to bring his racing heart under control.

Maybe what all of his therapists had told him was true. He wasn't ready to go out on his own yet. He tried to argue that everyone needed to stop treating him like a child, but now their advice seemed spot-on. His mind spun, his hands trembled, and his whole world tilted off kilter.

He slowly peered around the tree. Certainly the sound was just a car backfiring. That's what it had to be.

Or maybe it was a firecracker. Today was Saturday. Maybe some kids had been left home unsupervised and had decided to get rowdy.

But Riley's body wouldn't relax, wouldn't accept his reasoning.

Movement in the distance caught his eye. His neighbor, Mr. Parksley, emerged from the back door of his massive house. The trim older gentleman paused and looked around as if to make sure the coast was clear. Then he continued outside, dragging something behind him.

A rolled up carpet or rug.

An especially heavy carpet or rug.

Riley's throat tightened as he leaned into the rough bark of the pine tree.

Had Mr. Parksley shot someone and wrapped the body in the rug to dispose of it? The thought seemed ludicrous. Maybe Riley's brain was playing tricks on him. Maybe memories wanted to surface, and he was seeing things that weren't there, that hadn't happened.

Post-Traumatic Stress Disorder. That's what the doctors called it. Riley felt like he'd lived with it forever, when in reality it wasn't even six months.

One moment had turned his life upside down.

Mr. Parksley continued dragging the burgundy and beige carpet toward his truck. As he paused and looked around again, Riley scooted farther behind the tree. His heart still raced out of control as he considered the possibilities.

The fact that Mr. Parksley kept looking around was a sign that something wasn't right. If he were just a man taking his rug to be professionally cleaned, he wouldn't act so suspiciously. Besides, people in this area hired others to do this kind of work for them. Especially people like Mr. Parksley. The man had the largest house in the community and more property than anyone else in the neighborhood.

With a grunt, Mr. Parksley heaved the rug into the back of his truck. Several tries later, he managed to get the entire thing inside.

With one more survey of the area, his neighbor slammed the back of the truck closed, climbed inside the cab, and took off down the road.

Riley closed his eyes. What had just happened?

CHAPTER 2

After Mr. Parksley pulled away in his truck, Riley crept closer to the man's house. He had to know if he was going crazy or if something potentially deadly had really just happened. His sanity depended on it.

Dry autumn leaves crackled under his feet as he moved, the sound a sure giveaway of his presence to anyone who might be nearby. No one was around to hear except the squirrels and birds. Other neighbors were smartly inside their homes on this cold winter day.

Mr. Parksley's sprawling ranch-style house looked eerily still and without life. The lights were out, which led Riley to believe no one was home. As far as Riley knew, only Mr. Parksley and his wife lived there.

A worse thought occurred—what if his wife was dead? What if Mrs. Parksley had been rolled up in that rug?

The thought caused Riley's muscles to tremble, made his subconscious try to relive the day he'd almost lost his own life. He tried to push away the thoughts, to move forward as if the incident didn't affect him. He wasn't fooling anyone, though, not even himself. The incident hounded him now, trying to latch onto him. With every labored breath, Riley battled the flashes of panic.

His heart raced with every step closer he took. With one more glance around to make sure Mr. Parksley was nowhere in sight, Riley paused by the spot where the truck had been.

CHRISTY BARRITT

There, in a pile of leaves, was a brown shoe. It blended right in with the dry, crispy foliage on the ground, but it was definitely a shoe.

Riley squatted closer. Size eleven. Three inch brown heel. Jimmy Choo. It looked new.

He squinted, looking more closely. Was that a drop of blood on the top of it?

Riley pulled his phone out and took a picture. The shoe might not be significant, but he felt unusually compelled to capture the image. Staying focused helped to keep him grounded.

With the sun now below the horizon and grayness replacing the glowing orange, Riley crept closer to the house. He wasn't sure what had gotten into him. He wasn't usually the nosy type. But something about this whole scenario had gripped him and wouldn't let go.

With a touch of trepidation, he climbed onto the deck and approached the sweeping back windows of the home. Crouching down, he cupped his hands around his eyes and peered through the glass. Through the dim light, he saw a living room with high ceilings and neat furniture. Nothing looked out of the ordinary or indicated anything was wrong.

Riley continued along the perimeter, scanning the inside of the home as he reached each window. Maybe this was all a misunderstanding. He could have misinterpreted what he'd seen and heard. Maybe that hadn't been a gunshot, and instead his brain was going bonkers again.

Remaining low and hunched, he passed a breakfast area and reached what appeared to be the kitchen. He caught a glimpse of white cabinets decorated with roosters and placards saying things like, "Home Sweet Home" and "Love Makes a House a Home" above them. A large table blocked the rest of the view of the room, though.

He hopped over the deck railing and landed with a thud on the ground. He just needed a different angle. Balancing carefully on a wheelbarrow parked beside the brick veneer, Riley boosted himself up higher, daring to get one last peek inside.

This will put my mind at ease and confirm that something happened. Or it will prove that I have more issues going on in my brain than I care to admit. Neither possibility was comforting.

As his gaze skimmed over a kitchen island, his heart nearly lurched to a stop.

Blood pooled on the creamy kitchen tiles. Drag marks streaked outward from the puddle toward the back door.

The truth clutched at Riley, trying to take root.

Something had happened here.

Someone had been murdered.

CHAPTER 3

Riley's breaths came faster now, shallower. Panic pulsed at his nerves, wanting to claim his entire body. He knew he didn't have much time before his brain would be totally awash with something he couldn't control. He couldn't let that happen.

His hands shook out of control as he pulled out his phone. He had to call the police and tell them what happened.

He hit the wrong button, though, and instead of a keypad, an old photo appeared on the screen. A picture of him with his ex-fiancée, Gabby.

As soon as Riley saw her face, he sucked in a quick breath. Memories flooded him. It was more than memories, though—it was grief. Grief over what could have been. Grief over the fact that he should be married now. That he should be happy.

The phone slipped and landed on the grass below him.

Riley jumped from the wheelbarrow to retrieve it, scolding himself for becoming distracted.

Just as his fingers gripped the phone, a vehicle rumbled down the lane.

Mr. Parksley was back, he realized.

Before he could be discovered, Riley shoved the phone in his pocket and ran toward the woods. He'd call the police at home.

Otherwise, he might be the next victim . . . again.

***

Riley staggered through the back door of his house, barely able to get a deep breath. His mind—his body—still reeled.

His mom jetted from the armchair where she was reading and rushed toward him. "Riley, what's wrong? What happened? Are you okay?"

He leaned against the couch, trying to catch his breath and gather his thoughts, fighting desperately to remain in control. He had to keep it together.

His mom laid a hand on his shoulder, that same look of concern ever-present in her gaze. It had been there for the past several months, a constant reminder of what his family had been through.

"Mr. Parksley murdered someone," Riley finally said, his voice tight, strained. He took deep breaths, trying to ward off another panic attack. He couldn't afford one right now.

"What? Riley, you should sit down." His mom tried to lead him to the couch.

He pulled out of her grasp. "No, we need to call the police."

"You should calm down first, Riley."

"Every second we waste increases his chances of getting away with this!"

She frowned and reached for the landline phone on the end table. "I need to call your father . . . ."

"Mom—" Riley started. But as he said the word, pain jolted through his head.

He squeezed his eyes shut, trying to be stronger than the broken state of his body. It was useless. All he could do was press his hands against his temples and pray that the discomfort would subside.

Colors flashed through his mind. Blurred streaks with no discernable pictures claimed him. Each one felt like a blow and took his breath away.

Scum's face appeared in his mind, as sharp and vivid as if the man were in front of him. Scum was a notorious serial killer who'd tried to murder Riley as revenge for putting him in jail years earlier. The man had turned Riley's life upside down. Even though the man was dead, Riley feared part of Scum would always be with him.

He was the one who'd done this to Riley, who'd put a bullet through his head, one that was intended to be lethal.

At the thought, a moan escaped from him.

Then everything went black.

CHAPTER 4

Riley felt the leather beneath his fingers. Felt his heart beating out of control. Sensed the danger that lurked close by.

He jerked his eyes open, desperate to gather his bearings.

Where was he?

Had Scum gotten him again?

Images of waking up in the hospital flashed back to him, causing his body to revolt in pain.

Sweat covered his skin.

Then he smelled his mom's expensive perfume. Her face came into focus, and he noticed that her normally neat bobbed brown hair was tousled. Her eyes were lined with worry. Her knuckles were white as she wrung her hands together.

He was at his parents' house. He must have passed out.

When had he laid down on the couch? How had he even gotten here? And the bigger question: Why were so many things out of his control?

His dad peered at him, the grim lines on his face an unfortunate reminder of how tough reality could be sometimes. His dad had always been the strong one in the family. He was Vice President of a company that sold supplies to the Department of Defense. He had a tall, lean build, gray hair, and hazel eyes. People had told Riley that he was the spitting image of him.

His cousin Sophia, a nurse, stood in the background. She may have only been five feet tall and as skinny as she was

17

petite, but the blonde had a heart of gold. She'd been a huge support to the family, explaining all of the medical terms to them and often driving Riley to therapy throughout all of this.

How long had the episode lasted? Long enough for everyone to get here, Riley realized. What was that, an hour? Longer? Darkness peered in from the windows outside, signifying it was late.

He tried to push himself up, but Sophia appeared beside him. "You should just lay down."

That's when he remembered what had happened today. The gunshot. The body in the carpet. The blood.

"The police—" he started, jolting upright again.

Mistake. His head swam.

His dad shook his head and nudged him back down. "You need to rest, son."

"Someone was shot—"

Sophia squeezed his arm. "Riley, your brain is playing tricks on you. Repressed memories are trying to surface, and your reality is at odds with actual reality. This is perfectly normal for someone who's been through everything you have."

"I know what I heard, what I saw!" Riley's voice came out harsher than he intended. But he was so tired of people treating him like he was an infant. Yes, he'd been through something traumatic, but he wasn't going crazy.

His family exchanged looks with each other. And, again, Riley realized how little control he had of his life at the moment.

How have I gone from a successful lawyer about to be married to the woman of my dreams to this?

Why, God? Why?

With new resolve, he pushed himself up. The world around him wobbled again, but he ignored it as he reached for his cell. "I'm calling the police."

"Wait! Riley . . ." his dad said.

Riley paused with his fingers over the screen and stared at his father, waiting for what he'd say next.

With a grim expression, his dad finally nodded and raised his hand in a gesture of peace. "I'll call the police for you. We can put this all to rest."

"I . . . I have proof." Riley remembered, excitement zinging through him.

"What kind of proof?" His mom wrung her hands together.

Riley found the photo on his phone and showed everyone the picture he'd taken.

"That's a shoe, Riley," Sophia said, her voice soft and compassionate.

He shook his head, fighting frustration. "It fell out of the rug when Mr. Parksley dragged the body from the house."

Everyone stared at him like he was losing it.

Riley sighed and ran a hand through his hair. He sounded crazy. Even *he* couldn't deny that. But he *wasn't* crazy. How could he make everyone see that?

"There was blood on the floor inside Mr. Parksley's home," he continued, wishing he'd gotten a photo of that. Then maybe everyone would believe him.

"Did you go inside?" His dad's words sounded overly careful, and he appeared apprehensive as he stared at Riley. He sat in a kitchen chair that had been pulled close to the couch, leaning toward him and watching his every move carefully.

This home used to be comforting with its vanilla scent that lingered in the air and warm family pictures spread across the walls. Not anymore. He felt like a foreigner in a strange land being up here in Northern Virginia again.

Riley had to convince everyone that he wasn't being irrational. "No, I looked in the window."

"You were looking into our neighbor's house?" His mom's face went pale as she wrung her hands together again. "You can't do that, Riley. Someone's going to call the police on you."

Riley held up his phone again, aggravated—an emotion that was becoming all too common—at the lack of progress. "I'll call the police myself."

His dad raised his hand in that overly calm manner he was known for. "No, no. I'll do it. Everyone just needs to relax. We'll get this taken care of."

Riley watched as his father dialed the number, put the phone to his ear, and then wandered out of the room. Riley knew he'd gone out of earshot so he could explain to the dispatcher that his son had a brain injury and could be delusional.

Heat washed through Riley at the realization. He hated feeling weak and incapable. Even worse, he hated feeling sorry for himself.

They'll see that I'm not losing my mind. Riley couldn't wait to prove to them that he was more adept than they assumed.

CHAPTER 5

At eleven that night, someone knocked at the door. By then, Riley had drunk some water, eaten a turkey sandwich, and remained under everyone's watchful eye. It was like his family was afraid he might fly off the handle or do something irrational at any minute. Nothing would make him feel better except people realizing his claims were valid.

A wrinkled detective with bushy white hair and circles under his eyes stepped inside the house and introduced himself as Detective Gray. He took a seat on the couch while the family gathered around him.

This was the moment when Riley's family would realize he was telling the truth. Maybe he'd be able to regain some sense of his dignity. Maybe the feeling of unease would dissipate from his gut, from his tortured thoughts.

"I wanted to give you an update on your call," the detective said, his eyes volleying around the room until he connected gazes with each person. "We paid a visit to your neighbor, Wayne Parksley."

Riley held his breath, waiting for what he'd say next.

The detective's eyes fell on Riley. "I think you'll all be happy to know that things are well at the house, and there was no sign of foul play."

Riley stood up, alarm charging through him. "I know what I saw!"

His dad pulled him back down. "Just listen."

"We searched the house—Mr. Parksley was very open to helping us," Detective Gray continued. "There was no blood or any other signs that a crime happened there. I also searched our records and discovered Mr. Parksley is not a registered gun owner."

"But I heard a gun!" Riley said. He could feel the blood pumping through him, feel the urgency in each heartbeat.

The detective shrugged slowly. "Perhaps the sound was a car backfiring. You wouldn't be the first one to get the two sounds confused. It happens quite often."

Riley pushed away his aggravation and glanced at the detective. "Did you ask about the rug?"

Detective Gray nodded, and Riley saw that look in his eyes. Pity. Riley had seen it a lot lately. "Mr. Parksley was taking a load of items to a local thrift store. One of those items was a rug. There was also a bag of shoes. One of them must have fallen out."

Riley shook his head, which now pounded like a hammer. "No . . . "

The detective pulled his lips in a thin line before saying, "I appreciate your vigilance, but it looks like this was all a misunderstanding. Mr. Parksley is an upstanding member of this community."

"Let me guess: He even supports the local fraternity of police," Riley muttered.

"Riley!" His mom gasped, her hand rushing over her heart.

As Riley saw the astonishment in everyone's gaze, he backed off. He needed to sleep, to really think things through. Until he got his emotions in check, he'd never get anywhere.

But he knew what he'd seen and heard, even if no one else believed him.

CHAPTER 6

Even after a week had passed, the incident at Mr. Parksley's house kept replaying in Riley's head. Something had happened at his neighbor's that day. Riley didn't know what exactly that was, or how the crime had been covered up so quickly, or where the gun had come from, but something went down.

No one believed Riley. In fact, everyone looked at him like he was losing it. He saw the sympathy in their eyes. Even worse was when he saw the fear in people's gazes, especially his mom. She feared that something was seriously wrong with her son—that he'd never go back to being the way he used to be. Riley had been through a lot, but so had everyone who loved him. They'd all been victims in their own way.

"You okay, cuz?" Sophia asked.

Riley snapped his gaze toward her and nodded. He'd gone to church this morning with her instead of his parents. His folks had too many friends who knew what happened, which meant there were too many people at their church who patted him on the back and looked at him with that somber expression in their eyes. He couldn't take it anymore.

"Yeah, I'm just taking everything in," he said, casting one last glance around the sanctuary as people filed out. The place was still decorated for Christmas, which had taken place two weeks ago. Nothing about Riley had felt festive, though. Not being up here without Gabby.

At least he'd been able to hang out with Sophia today,

23

despite his melancholy thoughts. She always cheered him up with her sunny disposition. She was gentle, sweet, and one of the most nonjudgmental people he knew. They were only four months apart, and growing up, Sophia and her younger sister Olivia had felt like sisters. Sophia currently lived in an apartment only ten minutes from Riley's parents. It had been good to reconnect with her since he'd been back.

"How'd you like the service?" Sophia asked as they stepped into the lobby area.

"I have to say, it was refreshing." The sermon had been on the sanctity of life and how people need to treasure each day. He'd learned a lot about that himself. He had to admit that there were days when he didn't want to go on. He tried to pray himself through it, but he wondered if he needed something beyond prayer. Maybe his whole problem was that now that his faith was being tested, he was failing big time. Perhaps he'd been a fair weather Christian all along.

Whenever he went to church, it also made him miss Gabby. A highlight of his week had always been attending services with her and discussing the sermons afterward. Gabby always had a unique, honest perspective on things that he'd come to appreciate. She'd been more than his fiancé; she'd been his best friend.

"Riley Thomas?" someone called.

Riley paused before stepping outside and turned toward the voice. A figure from his past stood a few feet away. "Todd Andrews?"

His old high school friend grinned and stepped closer. The man had bulked up since their teen years, but otherwise he still looked the same. He had light brown hair cut close, a square jaw that seemed superhero worthy, and a wide-open expression that screamed "extrovert."

He grabbed Riley's hand and offered a hardy shake. "Good to see you, man. What a surprise."

"Yeah, what's it been? Ten years?"

"Since graduation, I'd say. You back in town?" His gaze flickered over Riley's shoulder and remained there a moment.

Riley shrugged. "For a little while, at least."

His gaze came back to Riley. "Last I heard you were practicing law. Are you still?"

Heaviness pressed on Riley's shoulders. Answering these questions never seemed to get easier.

"Taking a little break right now." Riley left it at that, not wanting to go into too many details. "How about you? What are you up to?"

Todd pulled his gaze from over Riley's shoulder again. "I was in the Navy for eight years. Now I own my own mixed martial arts studio. It's probably about twenty minutes from here. You should come check it out."

Riley nodded. "Maybe I will."

"Seriously, there's no better stress relief. We could all use that, right?"

Riley wondered if his doctor would approve. Maybe he would find out. The idea had its merits.

Sophia cleared her throat beside him, and Riley snapped back to reality. He was being rude.

"Oh, by the way, this is my cousin Sophia. Sophia, this is my old friend Todd."

"Pleasure to meet you," he told her with a warm smile.

Sophia's eyes glowed in return. "Same here."

"You should *both* come check out the place. First week's on me." He pulled out two cards and handed one to each of them. "I mean it. Plus, it would be nice to catch up."

Riley glanced at the card. The studio was less than a half a mile from his parents' place. That might actually be doable.

They said goodbye and Riley glanced at Sophia. Her gaze lingered on Todd as he flipped his keys in the air and stepped outside.

"He seems interesting," she said.

"Yeah, he is. He seems like he's doing well. I'm happy for him."

Todd had been a wrestling champ in high school and seemed like an all-around nice guy. He'd come from a rough background, but he'd risen above the low expectations other people had for him. It would be nice to catch up with him sometime.

"Want to grab some lunch?" Sophia asked, pulling her gaze away from Todd.

Riley nodded. "I do. But there's somewhere I want to stop first, if you don't mind."

***

"The thrift store? Really, Riley?" Sophia sighed.

Riley nodded. "I'm not working right now. I need to be frugal."

She stared at him like she didn't believe him. And for good reason. He had come here with ulterior motives.

The thrift store was only ten minutes from his house. If Mr. Parksley really had taken a load of items to be donated, this was the only location close enough to work within the time frame.

That meant that Mr. Parksley's items should be here. Better yet was the fact that this thrift store was independent, run by a local women's shelter. Other stores might send donations to a central processing location to be divvied up among various stores. Everything donated here should stay here.

"Oh, look at that purse!" Sophia's eyes widened with delight. "Is that a Coach bag?"

She wandered away, which gave Riley a moment to ask some questions without scrutiny.

Perfect.

He took a step and paused as the song playing on the overhead switched from something unrecognizable to "We're Not Going to Take It." His heart twisted with bittersweet memories. The song instantly made him think of Gabby and he could clearly hear her singing it in his mind.

So many things made him think of Gabby. Zany T-shirts, flip-flops, musicals . . . crimes. When would this ever get easier?

He shoved aside those thoughts as he paced to the front desk and offered his brightest smile to the employee standing there. "Excuse me. I'm looking for a rug. A good sized one for my bedroom. Maybe eight by ten. Do you have any of those?"

The older woman at the counter pushed her bright pink glasses up higher on her nose and studied Riley a moment. Finally, she shook her head. "Nope, sure don't."

"Are you sure?" Her answer seemed too quick, too easy.

"Yep, I'm sure. We keep all of the furniture and other items like that in the far left corner. If you don't believe me, you can go check for yourself."

Riley had a feeling that this woman knew everything that went on at this store. "Do you have rugs donated often?"

"Nope, can't say we do. Can't remember the last time we had one in here, for that matter."

"Have you worked here long?"

She nodded. "Yep. Eight years. Every day. That shelter saved my life. I've worked here ever since then. I've been looking for a rug myself, so I would have noticed if one came in."

"Certainly you don't work every shift, though. Someone else

could have been here when it came in and sold maybe?"

"Welp, I suppose Robin could have been working."

Riley's hopes soared again. "Do you know when she'll be working again?"

"Nope. She's been out sick all week." The woman stared at him, not offering any other help.

Spontaneously, Riley grabbed a pen and business card from the counter and jotted down his cell phone number. "When she comes back in, could you ask her to call me? It's important."

"This is all about a rug for your bedroom?" The woman was obviously on to him, and for good reason. This was a strange way to shop for a used rug, especially when there were plenty of other thrift stores around.

He shifted. "Someone I know said they dropped off a rug here, and this particular piece of carpet actually means a great deal to me. I know it sounds sentimental, but I'd really like to purchase the rug. I've got to locate it first."

The woman stared again and finally nodded. "Alrighty then. I'll have her call you."

Riley tapped the counter with his knuckles and nodded. "Thank you for your help."

As far as he was concerned, Riley had just proven that Mr. Parksley was lying. Sure, he needed to confirm the information with Robin, but the chances that his neighbor had dropped off the rug and someone had immediately purchased it were slim.

But what exactly had happened to that rug?

CHAPTER 7

After the visit to the thrift store, Riley and Sophia went to a deli just down the street to grab some lunch. Sophia, who probably weighed less than a hundred pounds, considered herself a foodie and often insisted on going to strange and unique restaurants. This one was fairly normal, if you excluded the Elvis Presley decorations that practically wallpapered the place.

They sat at a table by the window, and Riley stared outside at the gray sky for a moment. Sometimes he felt like he'd blinked and life had changed. Being up here near D.C. felt surreal, like he'd been transported into a different life.

"So, tell me about this Todd guy we ran into at church," Sophia said as she popped a chip into her mouth.

Riley looked away from the window, her question surprising him. "I went to high school with him. He always seemed like a good guy. He never did wrong by me, at least."

She raised an eyebrow. "Did the two of you hang out in the same circles?"

Riley shrugged. "I don't know if I'd say that. I was more into cross country and academics."

She let out a soft *hmm*.

"What?" Riley asked.

She shook her head. "You weren't the nerd you proclaim to be. As I remember, you were the golden boy without an enemy in the world, the one who could do no wrong."

29

"I don't know about that. I've made a lot of mistakes in this life. More than I'd like to admit."

"We all have. That's what makes life life."

He stared at Sophia another moment, deciding to change the subject. "Why are you asking about Todd?"

She shrugged and took a sip from her bottle of vitamin water. "I was thinking about that martial arts class. It could be a good idea."

"Maybe we should check it out."

"My work schedule is crazy for the next couple of days. But maybe after that." Sophia paused and frowned. Her expression easily gave away her thoughts.

Riley knew the conversation wasn't going to be pleasant. He'd known her since they were kids, and she always shifted uncomfortably before saying things she'd rather not say.

"So, we haven't talked about what happened at your neighbor's house last week," she started, using her napkin to wipe crumbs from her toasted tuna sandwich off her lips.

Riley shrugged, his meatball sub not looking very appetizing anymore. "What's there to say?"

"It's not uncommon for people with TBI to have episodes like that."

He'd come to hate the term TBI. He hated all of the labels people put on him. His therapist, Dr. Perkins, went especially overboard with her designations. He'd come to dread each time he had to meet with her. Somehow he always managed to feel worse afterward.

"It wasn't an episode," he started, knowing his argument would be useless.

Sophia frowned again, shoving the rest of her sandwich aside. "People are really worried about you, Riley. I even heard your parents talking about admitting you into the psych ward for a few days. I'm only telling you this because I don't want to see that happen. I really don't think you should push this."

He swallowed hard, getting her message loud and clear. If he wanted to continue with his recovery and receive favorable reports, he had to pretend he hadn't heard that gunshot. People thought he was going crazy, and he wasn't doing himself any favors by harping on it.

Gabby would believe him. She'd at least give him the benefit of the doubt. She was like that—one of the most selfless, honest, and determined people he knew.

The thought twisted his heart.

Riley remembered the first time he'd met her. She'd smelled like smoke—she'd been at the scene of an arson. There was ash in her hair and smudges under her eyes. She'd been the cutest thing he'd ever seen.

They'd both tried to prod a parrot down from a Bradford pear tree outside the apartment building Riley had just moved into. They'd practically been inseparable after that.

Riley missed her. Missed her intelligent eyes, the words that slipped out, her tenacity. Even more than that, he missed feeling her hand in his. He missed her smile that made him feel like a million bucks. He missed the possibility of spending forever with her.

Right now, Gabby wasn't here. She couldn't be here. He knew her well enough to know she'd give up everything to help him, and he couldn't let her do that. Riley couldn't hold her back when she had so many good things waiting in her future.

"Do you understand, Riley?" Sophia asked.

With a stiff neck, he nodded. He hadn't heard a word she said. "Yeah, I understand."

She leaned closer. "Riley, you realize who Mr. Parksley is, right?"

He offered a half-hearted shrug. "Not really."

"He's the former CFO of the very hospital where you're being treated. He's retired now, but people at River Crest General love him. Going around and bad mouthing him isn't a good idea."

Realization washed over Riley. This made it a little easier to see why people doubted his story. Mr. Parksley was an upstanding member of the community.

But that still didn't mean that Mr. Parksley hadn't killed someone.

CHAPTER 8

Later that day, after Sophia had dropped him off at home, Riley took another walk. His parents' neighborhood was lovely with large lots that had plenty of trees and houses that were as unique as the residents. All of the properties backed up to the pristine lake. Many had piers with gazebos at the end, and people often went boating in the summer. The area was located in Alexandria, Virginia, and was a nice retreat from the busyness of D.C.

He paused by the lake, his hands tucked in the pockets of his leather coat, and stared at the house in the distance.

Mr. Parksley's house.

He knew he'd told Sophia that he'd drop it, but he'd been drawn back to this place anyway. Apparently, he wasn't very good at dropping things.

As he stared at his neighbor's spacious back yard, the gunshot echoed in his mind.

His entire body tightened. Suddenly, he felt like he was back in his old law office. An image of himself at his desk filled his thoughts. He remembered his last day at the office. He'd been thinking about marrying Gabby, about beginning a new chapter in his life. He'd pictured what Gabby would look like in her wedding dress, what it would be like to share a home, how they'd eventually grow old together.

His lungs tightened as his thoughts turned dark. The last thing he remembered was a shadow crossing the doorway.

Then everything went black.

Eternally black, it seemed sometimes.

He found out later that a psychopathic maniac had stepped into his office and pulled the trigger. It had resulted in Riley being in a coma, fighting for his life. He had no recollection of that period of his time, though.

His therapist said that sometimes the mind shuts out traumatic experiences, but that it was a blessing because some memories were just too painful to remember.

His next clear cognitive moment was of waking up in the hospital.

In-between, there were several blurred images. He had the vague recollection of excruciating pain. He remembered bright lights and beeps and strange smells. But his first clear memory was of seeing his parents at his bedside.

Gabby had arrived at the hospital shortly after that. The effect of the whole experience had been evident on her face. Her lovely skin seemed paler than usual, her eyes more hollow, her movements more shaky. Riley couldn't even imagine what she'd gone through while he was out.

He'd only found out after he was discharged from the hospital that Scum, the very man who'd put Riley in the hospital, had abducted Gabby while he was in a coma. She'd tried to keep it quiet so Riley wouldn't worry and "hamper his recovery." Sure, Riley had been going through an ordeal. But so had she. She needed someone who could be strong for her, and Riley wasn't that person right now. He had trouble doing simple things for a while, things like paying his bills, remembering appointments, and even buttoning his shirt. He'd improved vastly from those early days.

He'd stuck around Norfolk for a month or so after being released from the hospital. But he'd had appointments every day with his occupational therapist, his speech therapist, his TBI rehabilitation physician, his neuropsychologist, and his physical therapist. The list was probably longer than that.

Of course, he couldn't drive himself anywhere, so he had to rely on other people to get him there. He'd had to rely on Gabby mostly, though a few others had pitched in. Losing his independence had been hard to stomach.

When he'd realized the strain everything was putting on Gabby, he knew something had to change. It was just too much for her. Riley knew she'd endure it, that she'd claim to be unbothered by the stress she was under, but he loved her too much to let her go through that.

After a lot of prodding from his family and talking to his therapist, Riley had realized the best thing to do was to come back to his parents' house for the remainder of his recovery. He could live with them until he figured things out.

He'd sublet his apartment to another cousin, Olivia, who'd just gotten accepted into culinary school in Norfolk. His parents had wanted him to end the lease, but he wouldn't do it. Letting go of his apartment would be too final, and he wasn't ready to make that kind of decision.

Leaving Gabby—breaking the news to her—had been one of the hardest days of his life. His heart had felt torn, and he'd second-guessed himself more than once.

But his appointments were a full-time job. *He* was a full time job, and that was the last thing he wanted. He wanted to be strong, a rock, someone dependable who made life easier for the woman he loved. The truth was, he'd heard the statistics. Dr. Perkins constantly talked about it.

Many couples find their relationships with each other change dramatically. Brain injury survivors often have new personality traits, challenges, fears, and limitations. This also means that many TBI victims behave differently in their relationships. Initially the changes seem temporary. However, sometimes these changes can last years. Divorce or separation is likely.

"Can I help you?"

Riley looked up and saw Mr. Parksley staring at him. The man wore a jacket, work gloves, and a faded baseball cap. He had a rake in his hands and a trash bag tucked into his back pocket, but Riley didn't see any piles of leaves anywhere.

Riley had drifted into his own world and hadn't even heard the man approach. Something close to fear tightened around his neck, began to swim through the murkiness of his mind.

He had to work through his rising panic.

After all, the police had said Mr. Parksley didn't know which neighbor had called the police. Since Riley and his family lived four houses down, there was a good chance Mr. Parksley didn't realize Riley had been the whistle blower.

Lord, help me now. Please.

"I'm sorry. I was just walking around the lake. I didn't mean to intrude." Riley wanted to ask questions, to prod, but he knew better. He needed to play it cool.

Mr. Parksley eyed him a moment. "You're Ron and Evelyn's son, right?"

Riley nodded and shoved his hands into the pockets of his black leather coat. He tried to look casual, tried to subdue the anxiety that threatened to control him. "I am."

He dipped his head in a sign of remorse. "Sorry to hear about what happened."

People often didn't know what to say to him. A lot of times they said the wrong thing. Riley really didn't need to be told that God had a purpose for this. Or that things wouldn't ever be the same. Or that no one really ever knew what life would hand him or her.

Riley knew those things and didn't need to be reminded.

But, as always, he nodded. Thanked them. Walked away. He chose courtesy over a knee jerk reaction.

Riley pointed to Mr. Parksley's house. "Nice place. You probably have the best view of the lake in the neighborhood."

He looked out at the water and smiled, the lines around his eyes deepening with wrinkles. "That's what sold me on the house. I'm retired now, and my wife and I might downsize. But this place has always been my oasis."

"Retired, huh? Sounds nice." There was a slight tremble in Riley's voice, as if his body and mind weren't working in sync. Evidence that his repressed memories were stronger than his willpower. That fact was hard to stomach.

He nodded, his breaths coming out in icy puffs. "Now I have time to fish and whittle."

"Whittle? Really?" Riley asked.

Mr. Parksley nodded. His hazel eyes didn't look like the eyes of a killer. No, he seemed like a grandfather. But that didn't change what Riley had seen and heard. If he doubted himself then there was no chance anyone else would believe him.

"Sure. I carve ducks, vases, bowls," Mr. Parksley said. "You name it, I've tried to create it."

An idea began brewing in Riley's mind. "I bet my mom would love something like that for her birthday. Do you sell your work around here?"

He shrugged nonchalantly, leaning on his rake for a moment. "Mostly I just make it for friends. Would you like to see some?"

Riley nodded. "Would I ever."

His pulse spiked as they started toward the house in the distance. He was going inside Mr. Parksley's place. He'd get to see for himself if anything looked amiss.

Riley could be walking into a trap, he realized. Mr. Parksley could know that Riley called the police and lure him inside to silence him, to eliminate the only witness to the crime.

The thought seemed so paranoid. But was that a real possibility? Riley couldn't be sure. Nothing seemed sure anymore. Regardless, his muscles tightened as his instincts kicked in. He had to stay alert and on guard.

His life could depend on it.

CHAPTER 9

Riley followed Mr. Parksley across the crispy grass, remembering when he'd walked this path not too long ago in order to peer inside his neighbor's home. He remembered the gunshot. The shoe. The blood.

As soon as he set foot on the deck, doubt crept in and he slowed. Maybe this wasn't a good idea. But he couldn't stop himself from continuing. He wanted answers.

Mr. Parksley leaned his rake against the brick exterior and rested his hand on the doorknob. "Excuse the house. I fired my cleaning lady last week."

The cleaning lady? Was that who died? But what kind of cleaning lady wore Jimmy Choos?

"Was she missing too many cobwebs?" Riley asked, keeping his voice light.

"No, but a few pieces of my wife's jewelry went missing. I can't say for sure it was Heidi, but not many people come into my home."

"I'm sorry to hear that. What company did you use? My parents are looking for someone now, and I'd hate for them to use someone less than honorable."

Breath in, breath out, Riley repeated to himself. He had to remain in control of his body and his mind.

"Wintergreen Cleaning. Use at your own risk, that's all I can say." He let out an airy laugh.

Riley stored the information away.

As soon as Riley stepped inside Mr. Parksley's, his lungs tightened. After crossing the living room, Riley lingered in the entryway to the kitchen. Images of that night flashed into his mind. So clearly, almost as if he'd studied a photograph for days on end, he could picture the blood there.

Had Mr. Parksley cleaned it up? Had the police used luminal to check for evidence the blood had been there? Even more troubling—whose blood had it been? The housekeeper, Heidi? His wife? Someone else altogether?

"Are you okay?" Mr. Parksley asked, peering at him from the fireplace.

Riley snapped back to reality and nodded. "I'm fine. My brain just doesn't work like it used to." He thought his cognitive abilities were starting to work just fine, but he would use that for an excuse for now. It was better than the absolute truth— that Riley thought his neighbor was a killer.

Mr. Parksley shook his head, taking his hat off and running his hand through thinning gray hair. "My friend in the police force got shot in the head during a drug bust. I remember how difficult it was for him afterward."

"How's your friend doing today?"

Mr. Parksley cringed. "Don't ask."

Riley already regretted that he had. He'd heard too many horror stories. While he wanted to face reality, he had to hang on to the positive right now.

"So, this is some of my handiwork." Mr. Parksley pointed to a shelf above his fireplace. There were all kinds of wooden ducks, a boat, a bear, and even a totem pole. Each was intricately designed with detailed lines and grooves and textures.

"I'm impressed." Riley stepped closer and examined one of

the ducks. "Are these the decoys that people sometimes use when hunting?"

"Not these, but that's how I got started. The ones I make now are more ornamental."

Riley glanced back at him, hoping his voice sounded light and curious rather than accusatory. "Are you a hunter?"

"I have been in the past. Not so much anymore. Now I whittle."

"I'd love to learn sometime, if you ever have a free moment." Riley wasn't sure where the words had come from. Whittling did have its appeal, truth be told. But he knew his motives ran deeper than that.

Mr. Parksley studied him for a moment. "Really? It's not something most young people are interested in."

"I'm not most young people."

Finally, he nodded. "I suppose I could teach you the basics."

His decision surprised Riley. Had Mr. Parksley's accommodation been sincere? Perhaps. But mostly it was made out of pity. Riley could identify the emotion from a mile away lately.

Of course, the man could have other motivations as well. Maybe Mr. Parksley suspected Riley was behind the phone call to the police and wanted to keep an eye on him. Riley needed to examine every possibility while remaining on guard.

"How about Wednesday?"

Riley tried to remember his schedule. Sometimes those details were the hardest for him to keep straight. He pulled out his phone and brought up the calendar. "I could be here after physical therapy. Say around three."

"Let's do it. It will be good. For both of us."

Riley nodded and forced a smile. "You're right. It will be."

41

CHAPTER 10

"Riley, did you have a nice walk?" His mom looked up from the kitchen table where she was working on a crossword puzzle and drinking hot tea with his dad. Her smile was a little too bright and overdone to be sincere. She was putting on a show, trying to make Riley think everything was okay.

Riley nodded as he poured himself some coffee, its rich aroma soothing him temporarily. "I did."

"Glad to hear that."

Riley leaned against the kitchen counter, contemplating ways to carefully broach the subject on his mind. He decided just to dive in instead. "I want my driver's license back, Mom and Dad."

He needed some independence. He needed to feel whole again. He knew he couldn't rush anything, but he needed to get on with his life as soon as possible.

His parents exchanged one of their worried glances. His dad finally spoke, "I don't know if you're ready for that, Son."

"I can be evaluated by the Driver Rehabilitation program. They should be able to say if I'm fit to get back on the road again or not. Of course, my doctor will have to approve also. But he says I'm progressing quickly, much faster than he thought I would."

"You really think you're ready for this?" his dad asked. A wrinkle formed between his eyes.

Riley nodded slowly but certainly. "I'm ready to take steps

42

forward. I can't keep living like this. I feel like I'm twelve again."

"I'm sure that losing your independence is difficult," his dad said with a deep frown. "It's going to take time before things start to feel normal again."

"Everyone handling me with kid gloves isn't helping me."

The silence felt strained between them.

"You can't rush things," his dad finally said.

"I want to get back to work as soon as I can. And I want to start taking a mixed martial arts class." He wasn't sure where that last part had come from, but it seemed like a good idea. If nothing else, the classes would keep his mind occupied and would help his body grow stronger.

Both of his parents stared at him like he was going off the deep end.

"Mixed martial arts?" his mom asked.

Riley nodded. "Todd Andrews has his own studio. I'd like to start there."

"The Todd Andrews you used to go to high school with?" his mom asked.

"That's right. I ran into him at church this morning."

"You'll need approval from your doctor," his dad finally said.

"I know that. I'll ask tomorrow when I'm at my check up."

If what had happened with Scum had taught Riley anything, it was that he never wanted to be unprepared again. He needed to be ready to fight for his life. Mixed martial arts would be a great starting place.

***

Riley's doctor gave him permission to train—albeit at a low impact and slow pace—and that very day his mom dropped him off at the dojo for the first lesson.

"Riley! Good to see you here." Todd sauntered toward him and clamped Riley's hand in his grip. "I was hoping you might take me up on my offer."

Riley shrugged, wishing he could think of a way to eloquently describe his thoughts. Instead, he shook his head and stated the truth. "Someone tried to kill me. If someone ever tries to do it again, I want to be more prepared."

Surprise washed across Todd's face. "Sounds like a good enough reason to me. Ever done any martial arts?"

Riley shook his head. "You might remember that I ran track in high school and college, and I used to play basketball with some guys for stress relief. But never any martial arts. I'm ready to learn."

"I do mixed martial arts here, so we do combinations of Ju-Jitsu, kickboxing, and karate. How about we get you started on the punching bag?"

Todd explained to Riley how to properly punch so he didn't injure himself. Then Riley put on his boxing gloves and began his workout. With each jab, Riley felt stronger. Working out relieved some of his pent up frustrations. The sweat felt good, and the exertion was invigorating.

"Good job," Todd said, bumping Riley on the arm when he finished. "You looked like you were really getting into it."

"It was good."

"It's hard to believe our paths crossed again, huh? Especially in an area like this. Who would have ever thought?"

Riley nodded. "Yeah, not me."

"God has a plan, though. There are no accidents. He's proven that to me time and time again."

Riley didn't say anything. To acknowledge the truth in that statement would be to also acknowledge the fact that God had a plan for Riley's brain injury. Riley wasn't sure he was ready and willing to accept that yet.

Just then, Riley looked out the window and saw his mom pull up. He waved to Todd. "I'll see you tomorrow."

"Sounds good, bro. I'll see you then."

CHAPTER 11

Riley leaned back in a leather recliner in his bedroom. He kept the lights low—the less stimulation, the better—and made sure it was quiet around him.

He'd spent the last thirty minutes trying to talk to God, but their relationship had come down to the most guttural level of communication—at least on Riley's part. Riley cried out to Him, not always having the words to communicate. God seemed to silently tell him to wait. Patience was not proving to be Riley's best quality.

As he closed his eyes, the gunshot at his neighbor's house resounded in Riley's mind again. He couldn't seem to stop thinking about it, even though he was determined to hide his obsession lest anyone think he was having an "episode" again.

He realized that he hadn't ever seen Mr. Parksley's wife, though. Not that day when he heard the gunshot. Not yesterday at the man's house. Never when he sat by the lake and let his gaze wander.

Could the man have killed his wife?

The only other possibility that came to mind concerning a potential victim was the cleaning lady. Mr. Parksley had said her name was Heidi. Perhaps she would be easier to eliminate as a victim than Mrs. Parksley.

While his dad was at work and his mom met with her book club downstairs, Riley did a quick internet search for Wintergreen Housecleaning. He easily found the company's number. On a whim, he gave them a call.

A woman answered on the second ring. "Wintergreen Housecleaning."

He cleared his throat. "Hi, I'm interested in your services and was hoping to get some more information."

"What size is your house?"

He glanced around his bedroom and tried to mentally calculate how big his parents' place was. "It's around five thousand square feet."

"How many bedrooms?"

He suppressed a sigh. He hadn't planned ahead enough to know any of these answers easily. He talked through the rest of the questions, wishing the conversation would move more quickly—specifically before his mom wandered upstairs to check on him as she often did.

The woman on the other line finally quoted an approximate amount.

"The price sounds decent," he said, even though he thought it actually sounded way too expensive. "Someone recommended one of your employees. Her name was Heidi . . . something."

"Heidi Klein?"

"Yes, that's it. Would she be available for the job?"

"I'm sorry, but Heidi is no longer with us."

Riley's heart raced a moment. "Really? I'm sorry to hear that. Let me get a few more quotes. Thank you for your time."

He hung up, his thoughts racing. Maybe it *was* Heidi who died.

But another thought also occurred to him. Why were there no other cars at Mr. Parksley's house on the day of the murder? If Heidi had died, then how had she gotten over there in the first place?

He shook his head. It was another mystery, he supposed.

He'd try and look up more on Heidi soon. But right now, he heard his mom's book club wrapping up. He needed to make things appear as normal as possible in order not to trigger any alarms with his parents.

With that thought, he went downstairs to tell everyone hello. He'd do more research when he had another moment alone.

***

"What are you thinking about, Riley?"

Riley snapped his attention back to Dr. Perkins. Dr. Perkins was a fifty-something woman with black hair that sharply contrasted with her pale skin. She always wore her hair in a severe bun, and the woman didn't seem to like smiling. Her gaze was intense, her blue eyes always assessing and labeling.

She was supposed to be one of the best psychologists who dealt with traumatic brain injuries. Riley had even started meeting with her before he moved back up here. Personally, Riley didn't see what the big deal was about her.

He shifted in his seat, so tired of talking. What would it be like if he simply canceled the rest of his counseling appointments? The idea was tempting, for sure.

He decided to be more honest than usual. "I'm thinking that I want to go back to Norfolk. Maybe coming back here was a mistake." The more he thought about it, maybe he could have made life work in Norfolk. He wondered how different things would be right now if he had. Maybe he could have asked more people for help. People at church. People in his apartment building. Maybe there were more options that he hadn't explored and his decision had been hasty. His brain had been in what felt like a permanent fog.

"Riley, coming here was the right thing. I think deep down inside you know that."

He shook his head. "I don't know, though. I don't want to be the kind of person who runs whenever the going gets tough."

"What do you mean?"

He didn't bother to fight the memories. Sometimes memories, no matter how painful they were, were a blessing. He'd learned that the hard way. "I mean that when I was right out of law school, one of my best friends died in a drunk driving accident. I turned my life around afterward. My relationship with God became real. I gave up being a defense attorney. Then after a high profile case, I realized being a D.A. was only a temporary gig for me. I moved across the country to start again. I don't want to keep doing that. I want to be someone who's stable, who's a rock. I feel undependable, and that's not who I want to be."

"This is about that woman again, isn't it?" She raised a thinly plucked eyebrow.

"Gabby. Her name is Gabby."

"We've been through this before, Riley." Dr. Perkins didn't sigh, yet her voice indicated that she wanted to.

"If moving here was the right choice, then why do I think about all the reasons it was wrong every day? Why does my gut feel so unsettled?"

"You can't trust your gut."

"Then what can you trust?"

"Your therapist."

Riley did let out a sigh this time. "Of course."

"Riley, you need to move on."

"I don't want to."

"Relationships after an injury like yours—"

49

"I know! I know." He'd heard it a million times. "But maybe Gabby and I aren't like everyone else."

"That's not likely, Riley. I know that's hard to hear, but it's better if you face reality. Your brain isn't working properly yet. Making decisions like this right now would be a mistake."

Coming to see Dr. Perkins always seemed like a mistake. He didn't voice that thought.

But he did glance at his watch. Thank goodness his time was up.

"I should go," he said, standing.

"Riley, the sooner you accept—"

He raised his hand to silence her. "I know. Repeating your advice over and over won't change anything. But thank you."

As he turned to exit, something on the shelf by her back door caught his eye.

It was a wooden bowl. And it looked just like one that Mr. Parksley would have carved.

Was that significant? Maybe not.

But maybe.

***

After therapy, Riley went back to Todd's studio. Todd offered to give him a ride home, which Riley appreciated.

It was another good workout, and Riley couldn't help but marvel that he should have tried mixed martial arts earlier. He liked the combination of moves, the exertion, and the way his thoughts became focused. What happened at Mr. Parksley's house always remained right beneath the surface of his thoughts, though.

"Want to grab a bite to eat?" Todd said, draping a white towel over around his neck. "I'm closing down for a couple hours before evening classes start."

Everyone else had filed out, and Todd had changed the sign out front to "Closed."

Riley dragged in a hesitant breath, realizing how nice it would be to spend time with someone outside of his family. "I'd love to. But there's something I need to do. Maybe another time?"

"I have a better idea. You need company?"

Riley glanced at his friend, wondering how much he could trust him. He'd always seemed like an upright guy. But what Riley was going to do seemed so out in left field that he was hesitant to tell anyone.

"Only if you feel like trekking through the woods," Riley started.

Todd raised his eyebrows. "Sounds interesting."

"Don't say I didn't warn you."

Ten minutes later, they climbed into an old Jeep Wrangler.

"Nice ride," Riley said.

"I'm pretty sure this is vintage now. Didn't seem like that when I got it my senior year of high school."

"You've had it that long?" Riley asked, looking at the well-maintained interior.

He nodded. "Sure have. Why get something new when what you already have works just fine."

Riley smiled. "Makes sense to me."

Riley gave him directions, and they started down the road. As the landscape rolled past, he waited for the questions to come from Todd, questions about what had happened in Riley's past.

By all appearances, Riley was fine. His hair had grown back. His skull was still even and not misshapen. To look at him, people couldn't tell the trauma he'd been through. No one knew about the turmoil going on in his mind or how his life had been turned upside down.

"Pull off right here," Riley said.

Todd eased off the pavement and onto the rocky ground along the street. This strip of road was secluded, leading into the quiet community where Riley and his family lived. The area was a haven away from busy city life, surrounded by acres of woods. Right now, the trees looked skeletal, with only a few surviving leaves hanging on for dear life.

After Todd put the Jeep in park, he turned to Riley. "Where next?"

Riley nodded toward the woods across the street. "Right over there."

Again, Todd said nothing. He simply opened the door and hurried toward the trees. "Are we looking for anything in particular?"

"A rug," Riley said.

He'd been thinking about it all day. Since Riley had essentially eliminated the thrift store, and Mr. Parksley had only been gone for less than twenty minutes, that meant his neighbor had to dispose of the body at a fairly close location.

Riley had seen Mr. Parksley's truck turn out of the driveway and knew this was the direction he'd come. He also knew that Mr. Parksley owned most of the woods on the far side of the neighborhood. This seemed like the most logical place to start looking for a body. After all, without a body, Riley had no case, and no one would ever believe what he'd seen.

He stepped into the woods, the ground moist under his feet. It had rained earlier this morning and the earth seemed to absorb all of the water. He glanced over at Todd's sneakers and had second thoughts. Neither of them had dressed for this.

"You sure you want to do this? I totally understand if you

want to go back to the studio now and forget you ever mentioned getting together."

"I'm curious now," Todd said. "It's not every day I'm asked to tromp through the woods looking for a rug."

Riley smiled. "It's a big rug, if that helps."

Mr. Parksley couldn't have dragged it but so far, especially through this terrain. As he climbed over fallen logs and squeezed between oaks and maples, Riley wondered if this was all a wild goose chase. But if not these woods, where else could the body have been dropped?

"So, Sophia is your cousin, huh?" Todd asked.

"Yeah, we're the same age, so she feels more like a sister at times."

"Seems like a nice girl. I've seen her at church a few times."

"She's great," Riley said, pushing aside a tree branch. "You been going to church there long?"

"About a year now. Ever since I got out the military and moved back here."

Riley glanced back. "You were in the military?"

"Until I lost my leg." He tugged up his pants until a prosthesis was revealed.

"I had no idea."

"Most people don't have a clue that my leg was amputated from the knee down, especially when I wear long pants. The whole ordeal gave me a new start on life. That's what I like to call it at least."

"What happened?" Riley couldn't believe he was asking that question. He knew how hard the questions could be to receive. Yet he was doing what he wished other people wouldn't do and inquiring more than he should.

"I was ambushed when I went into a village looking for some injured civilians. I was one of the lucky ones. Two of my guys died."

"Wow. I'm sorry to hear that."

Todd nodded. "Yeah. It was the deciding factor that made my fiancée break up with me. She couldn't handle the pressure."

Riley swung his head toward his friend. "That had to be tough."

"Better to find that out sooner rather than later, right? I guess I learned that if you find a woman who will stick with you through thick and thin, you need to keep her."

His words caused grief to grip Riley again. Had he made the wrong decision to come here? Should he have stayed in Norfolk and let Gabby sacrifice everything to help him?

Todd kept talking. "I was in the hospital for a while after that, learning how to walk again. I was really bitter for a long time. Then one day, I realized I could be bitter or I could make the most of what God had handed me. That's when I decided to open my own studio and get back to church."

Maybe Todd was right and it was no coincidence that Riley and Todd had run into each other. Had God ordained their meeting? He had a funny way of working like that.

Riley crossed the entire depth of the woods, reached the lake, and paused. He'd found nothing. Of course, Mr. Parksley may not have pulled off at the little patch of gravel alongside the road. It was the most logical place, but there were other acres of woods left to be explored still.

He glanced at the water. Had Mr. Parksley somehow anchored the rug and sunk everything to the bottom of the lake?

"No rug, huh?" Todd said.

Riley shook his head. "I guess not."

"Seems like this rug means a lot to you."

"Yeah, it kind of does."
"I hope you find it."
"Me, too."

CHAPTER 12

The next day, after Sophia took Riley for physical therapy, they had a quick lunch at an Asian fusion restaurant. At his cousin's recommendation, Riley ordered a General Tso's burrito, which was surprisingly good. As they ate, Sophia's phone buzzed, and she glanced at the screen before letting out a grunt. She picked up the device and began typing furiously, shaking her head as she did so.

"What's going on?" Riley asked.

"Gretchen, my supervisor, chose this week to take a vacation, which isn't a good thing because it means I have to deal with everything while she's gone."

"Is there a lot to deal with?"

She sent him a pointed look. "An investigation has opened at the hospital, if that tells you anything."

Riley raised his eyebrows. "Is that unusual?"

"I don't know if I'd call it unusual. I mean, there are lawsuits all of the time. People are always holding us accountable and blaming us for things that only God can control. But a lot of people are nervous right now over this one."

"Why?"

"Rumor has it that the FBI is even involved, and they'd been doing an undercover sting. Who knows? But as a result the hospital administration is clamping down on everything, which has made my job twice as hard."

"Sounds miserable. When's your supervisor going to be

back?"

"I don't know. She didn't even tell me she was leaving. But apparently she'd planned it because she filed all of the paperwork. She's like that. A lone ranger. Sometimes a jerk." She shrugged. "Anyway, enough about that. How are you doing?"

He nodded slowly. "Just fine, I guess. I went to Todd's studio a couple of times this week."

She tilted her head. "Did you? How was it? I need to go now more than ever. I could work off some stress." She glanced at her watch. "Speaking of stress, I should probably get going. I'll take a rain check on that answer."

"Sorry you have to drive me back." He hated feeling like such a burden.

"It's not a problem, Riley. It really isn't. I'm single, and I have nothing else to do." She shook her head, a slightly bitter tinge to her words. "Pretend I didn't say that. It's this time of the year when it's cold outside and you just want someone to snuggle with. Plus, I'm still reeling from the holidays. They somehow reinforced the fact that I'm alone. With each year that passes, my chances of staying this way increase greatly."

"You've never struck me as the type to be unhappy about being single." His heart ached as he said the words. It wasn't that he minded being single. He *hadn't* minded it, at least. Before Gabby. But after a person had met their soul mate, it was hard to go back to being alone.

"No, I think you can be single and happy. It's just that I have this biological clock that is ticking, and I want a family. But not enough to settle for someone who's not right for me."

Sophia had always taken strong stands when it came to love and romance. Just two years ago, she'd called off an engagement to a doctor because she didn't feel like their belief systems shared enough in common.

Her decision had been a wake-up call to Riley. At the time, Gabby hadn't been a Christian, and he'd seriously played with the idea of dating her anyway. When he heard about the struggles Sophia was going through, he knew he needed to wait.

He'd been glad he had. Gabby had been worth waiting for and he'd been amazed by the transformation going on in her life. She was an amazing woman. He only wished life had turned out differently.

"I hope you find someone and get that family you've always wanted," Riley finally said.

She smiled softly. "I hope the same for you, Riley."

***

Riley got home just in time to make his next appointment. Thankfully, this one had nothing to do with his recovery, though, and everything to do with his peace of mind.

He found his mom dusting the china cabinet, something she'd started to do on a weekly basis. Riley knew she was looking for excuses to be close by. His dad had even started bringing work home with him.

Growing up, his mom was always busy volunteering at church, having lunches with friends, going to Pilates, shopping, and everything else under the sun. That had changed in the past few months.

Everywhere he looked, someone was losing out because of him.

Riley paused in the living room. "Hey, Mom. I'm back, but I'm going out for a little while. I just thought you'd want to know."

She paused, dust cloth in hand. "On another walk?"

He shifted, knowing even before he said the words what his mom would think. "Actually, I'm meeting Mr. Parksley."

Her eyebrows shot up. "What do you mean, dear?"

"He's teaching me to whittle."

"To whittle?" she repeated.

Riley nodded. "That's right."

"This doesn't have anything to do with the incident last week does it?"

He shook his head. "No, of course not. I think the stress was just getting to me. I felt bad, so now I'm playing nice."

She nodded, and Riley thought he saw relief in her eyes. "I see. Well, have a good time."

He took off toward the backyard and followed the little path around the lake. Ducks and geese swam peacefully in the placid water. He was surprised they hadn't gone south for the winter yet. It was downright chilly out here, and Riley wouldn't be surprised if they got snow this season. The gray sky seemed to hold promise that precipitation was possible.

He tightened his scarf around his neck and reflected again on his conversation with Todd. In his own selfish way, it had felt good to meet someone else who'd gone through similar struggles. But his words echoed in his mind. *If you find a woman who will stick with you through thick and thin, you need to hold onto her.*

He could see how that applied to Todd. But sticking with Gabby would have meant essentially ruining her life. It would have been selfish of him to expect that of her. She'd even come to visit him twice, and each time he'd had to work hard at remaining at a distance. He'd felt like a jerk afterward. Maybe he was a jerk. But sometimes the answers for the future weren't as black and white as he'd like for them to be.

As if on cue, his phone buzzed in his pocket. He immediately pulled it out and glanced at the screen. His heart raced when he saw it was Gabby.

"Hey, you," she said.

Just hearing her voice made his throat go dry. "Hey, Gabby. How are you?"

"I'm hanging in. Staying busy, for sure. We've had to take on some part-time employees to keep up with our work load."

"That's great that there's no shortage of work."

"It helps pay the bills, right? How are you doing, Riley?" she asked.

He thought of a million things he wanted to tell her. He wanted to bring up Mr. Parksley and his mixed martial arts class and . . . basically, he wanted to share everything about his life with her. But he couldn't do that. Gabby would never move on if he didn't give her space. All he had to do was say the word and she'd be up here every spare moment, bending over backward to help. He couldn't let her do that.

"I'm hanging in. My life is basically therapy right now."

"I see. Is your recovery going okay?"

"The doctors have said I'm progressing nicely."

"That's great news, Riley. It sounds like you're really moving on." Her voice caught as she ended the sentence.

There was so much he wanted to say. He hadn't moved on. He hadn't moved on at all. But saying those things would only give her hope. He didn't want to do that. It was better if she forgot about him.

But why did his heart seem to say differently?

He floundered for a moment. Everything that came to mind seemed wrong. How could they have gone from sharing everything about their lives to this strain? He knew it was all his fault.

He spotted Mr. Parksley's house in the distance and paused.

"Gabby, I don't want to cut you off, but I have to run."

"I understand."

"I'll talk to you again soon, okay?"

"Yeah, of course." She didn't sound convinced, though.

That realization made his heart pang with sadness. And made him want to kick himself. Could it be that they were both trying to be strong for each other and, in the process, both were losing out?

He put his phone away just as he walked up to Mr. Parksley's house.

Riley knocked at the door and a man other than Mr. Parksley answered. "You must be Riley," he said.

Riley nodded. "And you are?"

"I'm Lockard, Wayne's friend. I just stopped by to drop off some venison jerky. He asked me to answer the door."

"You a hunter?"

He nodded. "That's right. Wayne and I like to go turkey hunting together."

Riley raised his eyebrows as surprise washed over him. Before he could ask any more questions, Mr. Parksley appeared behind Lockard. "Riley, good to see you here."

Lockard waved. "I'll be seeing you."

Riley's thoughts raced. Obviously, Mr. Parksley did have a gun. His wife also hadn't been spotted since Riley had heard that gunfire.

What exactly was Riley doing here again? Did he have a death wish?

He glanced at Mr. Parksley. A strange, unreadable expression lingered on the man's face. Riley hoped he didn't regret being here.

CHAPTER 13

"Alright. Sit down at the kitchen table while I get everything ready," Mr. Parksley said, sauntering off in the direction of the garage.

Riley did as he was told. But the blood he'd seen on the floor kept flashing back in his mind. He'd definitely seen blood here, evidence that something had happened in this room. Obviously, it had been cleaned up by the time the police arrived.

Riley glanced through the kitchen doorway and into the living room at the fireplace. Had Mr. Parksley burned the towels he'd used to soak up the blood? His soiled clothes? Was there any proof in this house?

Riley's lungs tightened. A tremble ran through his hands. His mind raced.

No, not another panic attack.

The attacks came at the worst times and made him feel helpless. No man wanted to feel like that.

A couple times he'd stopped the attacks using some breathing exercises Dr. Perkins had given him. He tried those now, breathing in to the count of three and then exhaling.

Even more than the breathing, though, he focused on praying.

Lord, help me get through this. I can't do this now. I know I'm broken, Lord. Physically, mentally, at times spiritually. I need You, Lord.

Riley jerked his eyes open when he heard movement behind him.

"We're starting your first lesson with a sweet potato." Mr. Parksley came back into the room with a box in his hands. "People are always surprised, but these little tater tots are the best for getting practice. They're soft enough to carve but firm enough to really get an idea for what wood will feel like."

As Mr. Parksley showed him some tricks and techniques, Riley somehow managed to stay in control. His trembles calmed. His breaths came more easily.

Until he saw the knife in Mr. Parksley's hand.

Riley's throat went dry as he focused on the blade.

If the man had killed once, he would kill again. All he'd have to do was jab that knife in Riley's direction and the second chance Riley had gotten on life would be gone.

That panicky feeling rose again, but he tried to push the emotion down.

Lord, I can only do this by Your strength. I beg you for that power now.

Finally, Mr. Parksley put the knife down. "Why don't you give it a try?"

Riley forced a smile, forced air in and out of his lungs, and willed his shoulders to relax. "Sure thing."

As Riley carved what he hoped would look like a face, he felt his heart slow. He was wasting time and needed to make the most of being here. That meant he needed to ask some questions, do a little digging.

He cleared his throat. "So, did you ever find a new housecleaner?"

Mr. Parksley shook his head, carefully watching Riley's progress. "Not yet. Good help is hard to find. Plus, I want my wife to have a say in it all."

"Your wife? I don't think I've met her yet." Riley tried to concentrate but ended up cutting off the entire nose he'd just tried so hard to carve.

He shook his head. "Probably not. She's down at some fancy spa in Palm Beach right now."

"Really? It must be some spa."

He let out a chuckle. "Yeah, you could say that."

"I'm surprised you didn't go down and play some golf. I've heard there are some great courses down there."

His face reddened. "Well, it just wasn't a good time for me. I just finished up my tenure with the hospital, but there are still a few loose ends that I'm trying to tie up."

"I heard you were an administrator there."

He nodded. "It's hard to let go of twenty years worth of work, even though I know it's time."

"Well, maybe next time you can join her."

His eyes still looked sad. "We'll see."

Riley looked down at his potato and tilted his head. Surprisingly enough, he could actually see a face appearing in the orange flesh.

"You see. You're getting the hang of it!" Mr. Parksley said.

Riley smiled. "I guess I am."

He stayed another hour and, when it was time to go, Mr. Parksley invited him over again the next day. Riley quickly agreed.

He'd do whatever he had to do to prove he wasn't going crazy.

***

After Riley got home that evening, he excused himself up to his room—his haven, lately. He looked up Heidi Klein on his computer. There were two people with that name who were listed as living in his zip code and both had phone numbers listed.

Should he call? If he did, he needed to formulate a plan for what he would say; otherwise he'd sound like a bumbling fool. He leaned back in his bed, trying to think it through.

Finally, he dialed the first number, but no one answered.

He tried the second number and a woman answered on the first ring.

He licked his lips, which were now dry. "Hi, I'm looking for Heidi Klein."

"This is Heidi." Her voice turned cautious. "Who is this?"

"My name is Lee," he said, choosing to use the second part of his name. Lies didn't easily roll off his lips, and he felt certain she'd hear the dishonesty in his voice if he strayed too far from the truth. "I'm actually looking for the Heidi who used to work for Wintergreen Housecleaning."

"Why?" The caution in her voice deepened.

The fact that she hadn't denied anything gave him hope, though. "I was hoping to utilize her cleaning services."

"Oh, is this Mr. Anderson? I guess you heard I got canned from Wintergreen. I was hoping some of my former clients would call and I could show that nasty Eileen Wintergreen that I'm a decent person. I get one client who claims I stole something, and I'm instantly the bad guy."

The good news was that Heidi was alive and well. The bad news was that Riley still had no idea if he'd really seen and heard what he thought he did.

"I'm sorry to hear everything you've gone through. I'm glad to know you've started your own cleaning business, though." He paused when someone knocked at his door. "Listen, Heidi, I've got to run right now. An emergency just popped up, but I'll call later about that job."

He looked up and saw his mom had peered into his room.

"Everything okay?" she asked. She asked that a lot lately.

"Yeah, everything's fine. Why?"

"I'm not used to hearing you talking on the phone. Not since you were in high school and dating Kelly Smithson. You remember her?"

Riley resisted the urge to roll his eyes. "Yes, I remember Kelly."

"She was such a nice girl, from such a nice family."

"She was nice. Gabby's nice too, Mom." He hadn't meant to say the words. But the fact was that he could tell that Gabby wasn't his parents' first choice. They wanted him to marry someone more like them. Gabby was from a blue-collar background. Her dad had been a drunk, and her mom had died of cancer. Gabby had pretty much made it on her own. Most people would admire that kind of tenacity.

"Gabby was very faithful to you, Riley. I could tell she cared about you very much."

"So why do you keep encouraging me to push her away?"

"Now, you know what the doctors have said—"

"But you were relieved to hear that was their advice. You were glad they encouraged me to take a step back."

She frowned. "We just want you to have more than we ever did, Riley. When your father and I first got married, we didn't have much money, and it was difficult. You always want more for your children than you've had for yourself."

"So this is about money?"

Her frown deepened. "She encourages you to follow your heart."

"Which is a good thing, right?"

"You'll never provide for a family if you continue with that law firm you started, Riley. You could hardly make ends meet taking on all those cases for people who couldn't pay you."

"Money isn't everything, Mom. I was doing something that made me feel good at a spiritual level." His parents went to church, and they loved God in their own way. But sometimes he still marveled that he was their son because his worldview felt so very different. He approached life decisions based on the Bible, based on prayer, based on the counsel of godly friends. His parents made decisions based on stability, financial freedom, and esteem from their friends.

They were from two different generations, and he didn't expect his parents to approve of everything he did. He certainly didn't approve of everything they did.

But, as soon as he could, he needed to get out of the house and make his own way. Staying here was only temporary. He was grateful for his parents' care and concern, but living here he was taking too many steps backward.

"If you ever want to have a family one day, Riley, you're going to need to make enough money to support them. Gabby brings out a different side of you, a riskier side."

"She encourages me to do what I feel called to do."

She wrung her hands together. "There's something your father and I want to talk to you about anyway."

Riley braced himself, his gut telling him he wouldn't like what she had to say. "What's that?"

"I should wait—"

"You've already started. I'd really like it if you finished."

"It's Jim Gleason at church. He's the managing partner at his law firm. He said he'd like for you to come work with him."

Riley let out a soft sigh, subduing the overwhelming emotions that rose in him. "Mom, you know I have no intentions of staying in this area."

"Where else would you want to go?"

"Back to Norfolk."

"For Gabby? Olivia said she's dating someone else. You've got to let her go."

He stood, surprise flashing through him. "What? You've got to be kidding. She's not dating someone."

"Well, she has a male caller."

"A male caller?" What in the world was his mom talking about?

"An admirer? Whatever you kids call it these days. That's what Olivia has said."

He sank back onto the bed and shook his head. Olivia lived across the hall from Gabby and would see everything going on. She would see everyone who came and went.

Had Gabby moved on that quickly? It couldn't be possible. He'd only been back up here for a couple of months.

"I know that's hard to hear. I'm sorry. But this position that Jim has talked about has a lot of promise. It would really help you get back on your feet again. You and I both know that you're in no state to start up your own law practice again. You're going to need some oversight as you go back to the real world."

Riley shook his head, frustrated with his life, with his parents, with the world, for that matter. "You've got to stop coddling me, Mom. I love you and Dad more than anything, but you've got to let me make my own choices."

She squeezed his shoulder. "Just think about it."

He didn't say anything. There was nothing he could say right now, so it was better to keep his mouth shut.

CHAPTER 14

Riley's mind swirled as he sat in the silence and solitude of his bedroom after his mom left.

Could Gabby really be dating already? The thought was so hard to stomach. He knew he couldn't have it both ways, though. He couldn't tell her needed space, and then expect her to wait for him.

He rammed his fist into the top of the recliner arm, trying to relieve some of his frustration. His life had not worked out the way he'd planned.

But that was going to change. He was going to push through with his therapy, prove to everyone that he was capable, and he was going to get his life back.

And it was all going to start with figuring out what happened with Mr. Parksley. It would help prove that he wasn't going crazy. Then he'd get his license back, look for a job, and push himself to overcome all of the obstacles that were ahead. After that, maybe he'd have a chance with Gabby again.

If she wasn't already dating someone else.

But if she could move on from their relationship so quickly, what did that say about what Riley had meant to her? None of this was Gabby's fault. He didn't blame her. He only wished his emotions didn't feel so twisted right now.

He sucked in several deep breaths, trying to get his focus. Thinking about Gabby and his mistakes in the dating department would only leave him frustrated and feeling like he couldn't do anything.

On a whim, he called Olivia. "Riley, wasn't expecting to hear from you."

"Just wanted to check on how things are going at my old place." Riley stood by his window, looking out at the lake and trying to tamp down his emotions.

"Great. Although your neighbor downstairs is a little strange."

"Sierra?" She was Gabby's best friend and an animal rights activist. Riley thought she was great, but knew she could come across as being a little strong willed and eccentric at times.

"No, Bill McCormick. I can't get him to stop talking about politics. Or his ex-wife."

Riley smiled. "That sounds like Bill."

"But Sierra is great. I've really liked talking to her. She's given me some great feedback on my vegan recipes. She's one very opinionated woman."

"She never minds giving feedback." His smile faded. How did he even approach this subject? He should have thought it through more. But now here he was. "How's . . . everyone else in the building doing?"

Silence stretched a moment. "Okay, I guess. The woman upstairs rarely comes out. And then there's Gabby. I guess you probably know about her, though."

"Know about her?" He leaned into the window frame as Gabby's face flashed through his mind. Her grin, her sparkling eyes, the determined raise of her chin.

"I assume the two of you keep in touch."

"Oh, right."

"I mean, she still has pictures of you up in her apartment, for goodness sakes."

His heart skipped a beat. "Does she?"

"You're acting weird, Riley."

"People have been saying that a lot since my brain injury."

"No, not that kind of weird."

"That kind of weird?" he teased. "Now you've got me curious."

"Oh, Riley. You really are the big brother I never had. I just mean that you seem like you're beating around the bush about something."

He let his head rest against the window trim for a minute as he tried to sort his thoughts. "Did you tell my mom that Gabby's dating someone?"

"Oh, that." She paused. "Well, I didn't use those words exactly. I just mentioned that a guy has been coming over to see her. I haven't seen them kiss or hold hands or anything."

"Do you know who he was?"

"I do. Garrett Mercer."

"Garrett Mercer?" Riley repeated.

"Yes, Garrett Mercer. Do you know him?"

"I received noticed that he'd bought our apartment complex."

"That, he did. I'm sure *that's* why he keeps coming to see Gabby." She chuckled at her own joke. "That idea is just absurd. The man's a millionaire. He has people who do stuff like that for him. I find it so odd that he bought this old, drafty building."

Riley didn't find it odd. Garrett had bought the building because of Gabby, no doubt about it.

"Listen, Riley, I'd love to chat more, but I've got to get to class. I'm making chateaubriand tonight."

"Of course. We'll chat more later."

"Oh, and Riley? Remember, your apartment is yours whenever you're ready to move back. I've got a classmate who said I can move in with her. I just thought I'd let you know!"

***

Riley couldn't resist looking up some more information on Garrett Mercer. He didn't like what he found.

The man was definitely a millionaire. He owned the Global Coffee Initiative, a company that donated money to build wells in impoverished areas for every bag of coffee they sold.

So, the man was rich *and* he had a big heart. Perfect.

Riley seemed to remember that Gabby had helped Garrett investigate what had happened to his family, who were killed in a mass murder when Garrett was in his late teens. Had the two of them bonded over the experience?

That was something he hadn't expected. At all.

The very thought caused Riley's gut to turn and squeeze. He'd never been prone to jealousy, but . . . he couldn't stand the thought of someone else being with Gabby.

Which wasn't fair of him.

But it was the truth.

He closed his eyes. He had to think about something else. Otherwise, he'd drive himself crazy. He'd told Gabby that he needed space, so he couldn't complain when she did just as he'd asked.

He tried to swallow the sour taste in his mouth.

Mr. Parksley.

Think about Mr. Parksley.

As strange as it may seem, thinking about a murder seemed like safer territory. He wanted to find answers. Maybe this was the resolution he needed to get back on track in the other areas of his life as well.

He tapped his chin as he mentally reviewed what he knew so far. His thoughts came screeching to a halt when he remembered that Mr. Parksley had said his wife was down at a spa in Palm Beach.

On a whim, Riley looked up all the spas he could find in Palm Beach. There were at least twenty of them. It was a long shot, and Riley knew that. But he didn't have much to go on here.

He narrowed them down to the most upscale ones with adjoining hotels. He'd start with those.

A perky receptionist answered. "Hi, I'm looking for Faye Parksley. I was hoping to catch her there. An emergency has come up at home, and I've misplaced the name of the exact spa where she's staying. I only know it's supposed to be the best in the area."

"You've called the right place then. Let me see if I can locate her for you. You say this is an emergency?"

"Well, that's not exactly true. But I'm her son, and my wife has gone into labor. She's going to be a grandmother! It's the only reason I'd interrupt her vacation."

"Of course." Computer keys tapped in the background. "I'm sorry, sir, but we don't have any guests who go by that name."

"Really? Because the Blue Lotus sounds like the place where she said she was going. Could you check one more time? It would make my wife feel so much better."

"Yes, one more time." More keys tapped. "No, there definitely isn't anyone by that name who's here right now or who's been here all week."

"Okay, I'll double check with my father. Maybe we had a miscommunication. Thank you so much for your help."

Riley hung up and frowned.

Then he called every other spa on his list, and they all said the same thing.

Interesting.

Had Mr. Parksley lied to him? By all appearances, he had. That might explain why there was no additional car at his house after the shooting.

But, yet again, Riley had to find proof. Just how was he going to do that?

***

Sophia picked Riley up for therapy the next morning. After grueling rounds of working his muscles, retraining his thoughts, and having specialists evaluating Riley for signs of progress, he was finally finished for the day.

"The doctors say you're doing really well," Sophia said as they walked to her car. "I mean, they can't tell me a lot. But they told me enough. You're progressing far more quickly than they thought you would. It's so hard to know with these types of injuries. But if you continue your progress like you are, it wouldn't surprise me if you were driving again in the near future."

Driving would mean freedom. Freedom would mean he could make plans for himself instead of being dependent on everyone else.

Hope surged in him.

"I was thinking about going over to your friend's martial arts studio. What do you think?" Sophia asked.

Riley blinked with surprise. "Todd's place? You don't strike me as the martial arts type."

She shrugged and hit her key fob. Her car beeped in the distance. "You're not the only one who can turn over a new leaf. I need some change in my life. I've been doing the same thing day in and day out since I graduated from nursing school. I need some excitement in my life."

He considered her words.

"I can't believe it's already a new year. Can you?" Sophia asked, climbing into the car.

"Not really." The holidays all felt like a blur.

"I know your parents really enjoyed having you home for Christmas."

"Maybe."

"They only want what's best for you, Riley, even if you can't see it all the time."

He chewed on her words for the rest of the ride. Did they really want what was best for him? Or did they just want what *they* thought was best for him? He'd had so many reservations about moving back home. But he'd had so few choices. His therapist had only solidified the idea, telling him how good it would be to have the stability of loved ones around him. He'd been reminded of how often relationships ended after TBI. And Riley had been exhausted. Spent. He'd reached the end of his rope.

He'd met with his pastor right before making the decision, and Randy had assured him that God worked all things for His good. But right now, Riley's heart felt so torn over Gabby. He wanted to let her be happy; but he also wanted to be with her. His thoughts volleyed back and forth from one extreme to another.

A symptom of his brain injury? He couldn't be sure. He only knew that he wished he could rewind time. He wished he knew back in August what he knew now. If so, he would have whisked Gabby off to get married on a tropical island, far away from the reaches of Scum, before any of this tragedy had torn their lives apart.

But there was no undoing the past, no matter how hard anyone wished for it.

They walked into Todd's studio just as class was finishing up and students were filing out.

"I guess we're too late," Riley said.

Todd met them at the front door. "I could show you guys a few moves."

"We'd love that," Sophia said.

That's when Riley noticed that she had her gym bag with her. She'd planned this in advance.

If Riley couldn't be happy and be with the love of his life, at least maybe his cousin and his friend had a chance.

Sometimes in life, you had to hang on to whatever good you could.

CHAPTER 15

After class, Todd, Sophia, and Riley went to grab some coffee together at a shop only three doors down from the dojo.

"So, Lily was asking about you, Riley," Todd started, raising his mug of black coffee.

Riley took a sip of his vanilla latte, trying to place her. "Lily?"

"You know, you met her at the studio the other day."

He vaguely remembered a woman coming in just as he was leaving after his first day at the studio. "That's right. The blonde?"

Todd nodded. "She's the one. I think she wants you to ask her out."

Riley shook his head and let out a weak laugh. "I'm flattered, but my heart is taken."

"You really like Gabby, don't you?" Sophia asked, her doe-like eyes gazing at him.

She'd heard about Gabby in the past. Riley had confided in Sophia more than anyone else since he moved back up here. She'd been his sounding board lately.

Riley nodded. "Yeah, I do. She cares about doing what's right. About following the call on her life, even if there aren't a lot of material rewards as a result."

"I see," Sophia said. "I can respect someone who does that."

"It sounds like you really love her," Todd said. "So why aren't you together?"

All the reasons flooded back to him. "Because it's not best

for her right now. I don't want to be a burden."

"If she's as great as you said she is, then it sounds like she wouldn't mind," Todd said.

"She probably wouldn't, but I do. I've got to get myself straight."

Todd nodded. "I'll pray about it for you, man. Love is one of those things you don't ever want to regret. I wish I had had someone beside me after my stint in rehab."

"Wait a minute, Riley." Sophia narrowed her eyes. "I've never asked, but what reason exactly did you give Gabby for moving back up here? I assumed it was because of therapy and that something else had happened to cause you two to break up."

"Well, it was because of therapy. And it was because I care about her too much to see her forgo all of her plans for me."

Sophia's mouth dropped open. "I love you, cuz, but you've got to be the biggest idiot ever."

Her words felt like a smack in the face. "What are you talking about? I only left because I love her! I decided to sacrifice my happiness so she could ultimately be happy. She won't be happy with me. I'm too . . . broken." The words didn't feel good leaving his lips. But wasn't it the truth? She would be better off without him holding her back.

"Does she know you feel that way?"

He shook his head.

"Of course not. You're trying to be chivalrous and noble, but in the meantime she's broken hearted, thinking you ditched her at the first opportunity. She was there for you and willing to hold on to the end. What did you do? You left her. That's her perspective."

Riley's jaw tightened. "It wasn't like that."

"Besides, are you sure you weren't afraid of being rejected

by her?" Sophia continued. "That you didn't have some deep seated fears about not appearing strong and manly? Motivations are rarely as simple as we'd like. I think you hit the nail on the head when you said you were too broken for her. I can guarantee you, you're not."

Riley started to speak but stopped himself. What if Sophia was right? If she was, then he'd made the biggest mistake of his life. "I really thought I was doing what was best for her."

"You need to tell her that. Stop trying to be the good guy all the time and fight for what you want."

He shook his head, finding reality harder and harder to swallow by the minute. "It's too late. She's dating someone."

"I doubt she's really dating someone," Sophia said. "You can't go from a relationship like yours to being in love with someone else like that."

Todd nodded. "It's true. I'm just now getting to the point where I feel like I could date. You have no idea what you have." He cringed. "Had? Anyway, there was nothing I wanted more than for my fiancée to stick by me when the going got tough. But an injured spouse wasn't in her long-range plans."

"That sounds terrible," Sophia said, frowning as she turned all of her attention on Todd.

"It was hard. But God has a plan, right?"

She smiled softly. "That's right. He does. Even when we don't see it. Life, no matter what happens, is precious."

"By the way, are you going to that Bible study on Wednesday nights at church . . . ?"

As they broke off into their own conversation, Riley's thoughts drifted. God did have a plan, no matter how hard it was to see. Riley only hoped that plan would be revealed soon because he was losing hope quickly.

Especially after his conversation about Gabby. He'd really

screwed up, hadn't he? Even worse, it was probably too late to do anything about it. Besides, the truth remained ingrained inside him that, despite how hard this was, what he'd done had been for the best.

Not his best, but Gabby's best.

Because sometimes, loving someone meant letting them go.

CHAPTER 16

Later that day, Riley knocked at Mr. Parksley's door. He opened it a moment later and smiled when he recognized Riley. "You're early."

"Hope you don't mind." He held up the sweet potato project he'd finished last night as he stepped inside. "Everyone was quite impressed with my George Washington head."

"George Washington? I thought it was a jack-o-lantern." He smiled, and Riley realized he was teasing.

"I'll have you know, I spent hours on this."

"You'll get better." He indicated for Riley to follow him.

Riley glanced around as he walked through the house. Everything appeared in place, with or without his maid or wife being here. Mr. Parksley was obviously a very tidy person. Tidy and detailed enough that he'd been able to clean up after a murder without anyone being the wiser?

"Have a seat at the kitchen table while I get my things," Mr. Parksley said.

Riley didn't sit, though. He lingered by the kitchen counter, images hitting him again. In his mind, he saw the blood on the floor. He saw the puddle. He saw the streaks coming from it.

What had happened in this room?

He leaned against the kitchen counter, trying to stay in control.

Lord, please help me! I can't get through this without You.

He never knew when panic and anxiety would come or what

would trigger it. He closed his eyes and tried to steady his breaths.

A moment later, he opened his eyes, his heart slowing. He could do this. He just had to keep breathing, keep praying, keep focusing.

His eyes fell on some papers left on the kitchen counter.

Faye Parksley's name was there.

Last week's date peeked out from the corner.

At the top, he could see the letters "ling center."

He started to shove aside the papers on top when Mr. Parksley came back into the room.

"You ready to get started?"

"Am I ever!" he said a little too brightly.

He sat at the table and Mr. Parksley gave him additional pointers on carving the sweet potato. As the man talked and told stories about some of his first projects, Riley's mind kept going back to that day he'd heard the gunshot.

His gaze drifted to the kitchen floor. Had there been a rug there at one time? He couldn't be sure. The floor space was big enough for one.

He squinted. If he looked closely enough, the center of the kitchen floor did look glossier than the rest, like maybe it had been protected from the normal wear and tear of foot traffic.

Suddenly, something sharp hit his finger. Looking down, he spotted blood on his index finger. He'd gotten distracted and the knife had nicked him.

"A lot on your mind?" Mr. Parksley asked, rising to grab a paper towel.

Riley spine tightened. There was no malice behind his words. It was just a simple question. "I guess so. My brain doesn't quite work the same way it used to."

"Brain injuries take time. Don't rush yourself."

He nodded and put the paper towel over his finger. "Could I use your bathroom for a moment?"

"Second door on the left," Mr. Parksley said.

Riley's hands shook as he started down the hallway. He paused at the bathroom door and gazed down the length of the hallway. One door was open.

Could that be Mr. Parksley's bedroom? If this house was anything like Riley's parent's place, then the master suite was on the first floor.

He pushed aside his scruples for a moment and tiptoed down the hall. He nudged the door at the end and a large bedroom came into sight.

This had to be the master suite.

A plan—hasty, as it was—formed in his mind. It was a long shot, but a risk that could pay off. He had to hurry, though.

He rushed across the room and opened the first door he saw. Men's clothing stared back at him. This wasn't the right closet.

Wasting no time, he opened the next door.

This was it.

This was Faye's closet.

He knelt down and picked up one of her shoes. He had to see what size she wore.

It was a . . . six? What? That couldn't be right.

The shoe he'd found was a size eleven. If this was right then that shoe he'd seen in the leaves didn't belong to Faye.

He put it back where he found it, facts sloshing together in his mind.

"Riley?"

Riley jerked his head up. Mr. Parksley stood in the doorway, staring at him.

"This isn't the bathroom," Riley started.

"No, it's not." He stared at him, leeriness in his gaze.

"I'm sorry. It's my brain injury. I . . . I don't know what to say." He hated to use his TBI as an excuse, but if there was any time to do it, it was now.

Mr. Parksley still eyed him critically. "Are you okay?"

He ran a hand through his hair. "You know what? I think I should lay down. I hate to cut this short, but I feel like I should head home."

"Do you want me to drive you?"

Riley shook his head. "No, I'm going to walk. The fresh air will be good for me."

Before Mr. Parksley could say anything else, Riley apologized again and was out the front door.

He had a lot of thoughts to sort out.

WHILE YOU WERE SWEEPING

CHAPTER 17

"Are you okay, dear?" his mom asked.

He was really getting tired of her asking that.

Riley dropped into a chair at the kitchen table and nodded, his thoughts racing a mile a minute. "I'm fine, Mom."

"Can I get you some coffee?"

He nodded. "That actually sounds great."

While she walked across the kitchen, Riley glanced down at the newspaper. The headline read, "River Crest Hospital under Investigation."

This must be what Sophia had talked to him about when she'd mentioned all of the stress at work and the scrutiny the staff was under. Mr. Parksley was probably glad he'd gotten out when he had.

His mom set some coffee in front of Riley and then lowered herself across from him. "How was whittling?"

He nodded. "It was fine."

She gasped and pointed to the bloody tissue on his finger. "What happened? Are you okay?"

"Just a little cut. It's fine. I promise."

"Are you sure—?"

He held up his hand. "Mom, I'm fine. Really."

She stared at him several minutes before nodding. "Where's your latest creation?"

He looked down and realized his hands were empty— except for the bloody napkin. "I didn't finish it yet. I'll have to go back and work on it some more."

"I see."

Riley leaned back. "Mom, what's Mrs. Parksley like? I've yet to meet her."

"She's a strange one. The opposite of her husband. He's always been quiet and private. A numbers guy. She's gregarious and social and always in people's business. They're living proof that opposites attract."

"I take it she doesn't work?"

"She doesn't work that I know of. She's too busy having cocktails with her friends. She likes her wine a little too much, if you know what I mean."

"She's an alcoholic?" Riley questioned.

"It wouldn't be very nice for me to conjecture. But that's the rumor. In fact, the last time I saw her, I ran into her at a grocery store. She seemed three sheets to the wind, even then."

An idea suddenly hit. "Mom, can you excuse me a minute?"

"Of course."

Riley hurried up to his room. On a whim, he typed in "Palm Beach Rehab Centers."

Sure enough, Serene Waters Healing Center popped on the screen.

That's where Faye was, wasn't it? The letters fit with what Riley had read on that sheet of paper on Mr. Parksley's kitchen counter. She'd gone to rehab and Mr. Parksley was telling everyone she was at a spa to save her the embarrassment.

It made sense.

He sighed.

But if Riley was right, that left him right back at square one. It wasn't Heidi, the maid. It wasn't Faye, the wife.

Then who else could it be?

Riley had no clue.

Maybe he was going crazy. Maybe all of this was a misunderstanding.

Even worse, he didn't even *want* Mr. Parksley to be guilty. The man was nice. He sensed honesty in the man's eyes.

But he also sensed something unsettled about him, that he had a secret.

He desperately needed someone to talk to about everything. But every person he encountered caused some type of roadblock to go up. He had a million excuses why he couldn't talk to them, why they'd only pat him on the shoulder and cast him those looks of sorrow. He wouldn't put himself through that.

But there was one person who came to mind, and he couldn't help but think she'd understand. She'd get it. She'd get him.

Gabby.

He stared at his phone again, his thoughts clashing inside.

She was dating someone else. If he called her now, would he ruin her chances for happiness? Would he be stringing her along? Doing the ultimate injustice to her?

He didn't know.

And, for that reason, he put his phone away. He still had some things to work out before he could take any action.

***

That night as he lay in bed trying to sleep, his cell phone rang.

His heart raced in anticipation.

Could it be Gabby?

Instead, it was Gabby's best friend, Sierra.

Riley frowned. Why was she calling? Sierra never called him.

He answered quickly, his thoughts turning from curious to worried. "Sierra?"

"Hello, Riley," she said, her voice crisp and professional. "How are you?"

He sat up in bed, confusion washing through him. There was absolutely no urgency or concern in her voice. What was this about? "I'm hanging in. You?"

"Doing quite well, thank you."

"Is everything okay?"

"Gabby is having a hard time, and I don't like it," she blurted.

His heart twisted. "What do you mean?"

"I mean, I hate seeing her so heartbroken like this."

The knife in his heart twisted even deeper. "Did something happen? Do I need to go down there? Is she okay?"

"You left her broken hearted, so you tell me."

His spirit sank, and he let his head fall back against the headboard behind him. This was about him moving away. First he'd heard it from Sophia, now Sierra. Was God trying to tell him something? "Sierra, it's complicated."

"I know. Life is complicated. I've been telling her to wait for you, but I'm not sure I'm going to do that anymore. I don't want to see her get jerked around."

"I'm not trying to jerk her around."

"That's sure what it feels like."

"Sierra—" he started.

"There's a nice guy who's interested in her. I think she should date him."

Riley clamped his mouth shut. Sierra had always been one of Gabby and Riley's biggest supporters. To hear those words leave her mouth felt like a slap on the face. "Garrett Mercer?"

"Yes, Garrett Mercer."

He swallowed hard, trying to find the right words. "Sierra, I care about Gabby deeply."

"She cares about you, as well. But after that last visit, I just can't stand to see her hurting as she is."

"What happened during our last visit?" Had he forgotten something? He searched his memories, but came up with zero. Gabby had come up for the day, she'd had dinner with his family, they'd taken a walk and talked about therapy. That had been right before Christmas.

"Oh, I don't know. Your mom told her not to come up and visit anymore, maybe."

"What?" He nearly jumped out of his bed. "What are you talking about?"

"Your mom told Gabby that you seemed more upset every time after you saw her. She asked her not to come up anymore."

Anger burned in him. So that's why Gabby had backed off. She'd definitely seemed more distant lately, and all along he'd been clueless about the real reason why.

"I didn't know that, Sierra. My mom failed to mention that little talk with Gabby to me."

"Well, it happened. Please don't hurt her anymore, Riley," Sierra said. "She deserves better."

He chomped down. "I won't, Sierra. That was never, ever my intention. I only want what's best for her. Right now, I'm not sure if that's me."

"Well, make up your mind or you might lose her forever."

Riley hung up and stared off into space for a moment. How could his mom have interfered like this? She'd had no right. This was hard enough without curveballs like this.

That settled it in his mind. As soon as possible, he was

moving out. Right now, he needed to talk to his parents, though.

CHAPTER 18

"How could you do that, Mom?" Riley asked, trying his best to keep his tone respectful.

"I only want what's best for you, Riley. You've got to understand that." She frowned again.

"Why does everyone else get to determine what's best for me?"

"Son, you need to calm down," his father said.

They both looked sleepy and wore their pajamas as they sat on the couch and watched the news, their nightly ritual. Neither of them probably ever thought his mom's words would get back to Riley.

"I'm tired of calming down. I'm tired of trying to be a good little patient and son and everything else people want me to be. I'm an adult. Sure, I have some issues I'm working through, but I deserve the chance to make my own decisions. I understand that I have to live with the repercussions of those, but that's what life is about."

He expected them to argue. Instead, they remained silent for several moments. Finally, his mom nodded. "You're right. You do deserve control your own life. I have overstepped my boundaries. But I only did it because I love you."

He was beyond tired of that reasoning. "Why would you say that to Gabby? I just don't understand."

"You did seem upset after her visit," his mom said.

"Of course I was upset. I miss her. I miss my old life. I may have a brain injury, but I'm not incompetent."

Riley's father reached for the phone. "I should call Dr. Perkins—"

"Absolutely not. I'm done with Dr. Perkins. I'm done with living like this. I can't do it anymore." He started back toward his room.

"Where are you going?" his dad called.

"Figuring out how to take control of my life back."

***

Riley went to the hospital with Sophia the next day, but he purposefully skipped his appointment with Dr. Perkins. He'd had enough of her. Instead, he wandered the hospital halls. There definitely seemed to be some tension in the air. The investigation going on here had put the staff on edge and their security measures had been tightened.

He paced down to the administrative area of the hospital. As he got closer to the doorway leading into the area, two men in suits stepped out.

The FBI maybe? Something about the way they carried themselves gave him that impression. If he was right, this investigation really was a big deal.

Riley paused a moment. This was where Mr. Parksley had worked, here in this area. He would have been privy to what was going on at the hospital and the allocation of funds—or missing funds, for that matter. Could all of this tie in with the investigation somehow?

He wasn't sure. But it beat his other theories—which were nonexistent at this point.

He stepped inside the administrative area. The front desk was empty so he wandered toward the offices in the back. He stopped by the doorway with the blank nameplate outside.

Could this be Mr. Parksley's old office? Riley had heard they hadn't found anyone to replace him yet. He glanced around.

All the other offices had names on the doors.

"Can I help you?" a petite woman with short salt and pepper hair asked.

He swallowed, quickly formulating his thoughts. "I was looking for Wayne Parksley."

The woman offered a clipped smile. "I'm sorry. He's retired."

"I see. Well, I was actually trying to locate his secretary. When I was here last, she had this wooden bowl in her office, and I wanted to ask where she got it. My mom has a birthday coming up and I think she'd love one." He remembered the bowl he'd seen in Dr. Perkin's office. Maybe Mr. Parksley made it a habit to give them out to people here at the hospital.

"I'm sorry. She's . . . she's out right now." She shifted uncomfortably.

"Do you know when she'll be back?"

The woman shook her head. "I'm sorry. I don't. Vicki has been out for a couple of weeks now."

"Out for a couple of weeks? Wasn't that interesting. Could this somehow tie in with the gunshot he'd heard at Mr. Parksley's? The timeline fit.

"I see," he said again. "Well, thank you for your help."

He wanted to find Sophia and ask her a few questions. Before he even made it to the second floor where she was working, someone called to him from down the hallway. "Riley Thomas!"

He turned and saw Dr. Perkins. Dread filled him as he waited for her to catch up. "You skipped our appointment today?"

He nodded. "I did."

"This could seriously delay your recovery. These appointments are very important."

"I'm finding a new psychologist, Dr. Perkins."

Her lips parted. "Are you? Why would you want to start over like that?"

"Because I want someone who will acknowledge my faith as the hope I have in recovering. I want someone who understands the importance of my relationships and doesn't encourage me to break things off with the people I love."

"I was only being realistic."

"Your 'realistic' isn't the same as mine." He paused and nodded toward the elevator. "Now, if you'll excuse me."

Before she could say anything else, he hurried upstairs and found Sophia at the nurse's station.

"What's going on?" Sophia asked, gathering some charts.

He walked down the hallway with her as she hurried to a patient's room. "What do you know about Vicki down in the administrative office?"

"I don't even think I know her. Why?"

"No one has seen her for a couple of weeks."

She stopped and tilted her head. "Is this about what happened at Mr. Parksley's? I thought you were going to drop this?"

"Maybe she had something to do with the investigation at this hospital. Maybe she and Mr. Parksley both did."

Sophia shook her head. "I don't know what to say. I don't know her, so I can't really help. And I've got to get to my patient's room. I'll give you a ride home on my lunch break, okay?"

He bit back disappointment at her easy dismissal. "You know, I think I'm going to catch a cab today. You seem busy."

"Are you sure?"

Riley nodded. "Positive."

Feeling like he'd reached another dead end, he started down the hallway. Maybe this was a wild goose chase. All of his supposed clues had led him nowhere.

"Excuse me!" someone said in a loud yet hushed voice.

He pivoted until he saw a woman down the adjoining hallway. She was a middle-aged black female with bright eyes and big movements. She also wore a hospital badge.

She waved him over, her gaze searching her surroundings as she did so, as if she feared being caught. Riley hesitated before stepping toward her.

"Yes?"

"Were you asking about Vicki?" she whispered, leaning close.

He remained cautious as he nodded. The woman didn't appear to be a nurse, but she did have some type of uniform on. "I was."

"Rumor has it that a missing person's report has been filed."

"How do you know this?"

"I work in the cafeteria. I used to talk to Vicki every day. I noticed she was gone, so I started asking questions. I thought it was weird, you know?"

Riley nodded. "And you actually heard about that missing person's report?"

"I did. From someone else in the office. They're trying to keep it all hush, hush in light of everything else going on at the hospital right now." She shrugged. "Anyway, I heard you asking about her as you walked past. I'm tired of the secrets around here, so I decided to speak my mind. Just don't tell anyone."

"Any rumors about what may have happened?"

"Some people think she's involved in this scandal here at

the hospital and that she ran away. Other people think she was having trouble at home. Only she knows the truth, and she's nowhere to be found."

He nodded. "Okay. Thank you for your help."

Maybe Riley wouldn't be going straight home after all.

CHAPTER 19

Riley stared out the window as the landscape rolled past. For some reason, his future seemed to pivot on him solving this case. Not in anyone else's mind except his own. But finding out who died felt like it would redeem him in some way. It would prove that he wasn't going crazy.

But just how would he do that?

He couldn't live under the suspicion of everyone thinking he was crazy for the rest of his life. Because, if he did, he had no hope of returning to his career as an attorney. No one would want someone they perceived as irrational representing them.

It seemed like everything that was important to him was being stripped away. His job. Gabby. His home.

The only thing he had to hang onto was his faith, and even that seemed a bit slippery at times.

As the taxi took him closer to his home, a familiar truck pulling out in the distance caught his eye.

It was Mr. Parksley.

And he was leaving the thrift store.

"Wait! Stop here for a minute," he told the driver.

They pulled into the parking lot.

Just what was Mr. Parksley doing here? Riley needed to find out. It could be nothing.

Or it could be everything.

Riley walked around toward the donation drop off area

where he'd seen the truck come from. He stopped in his tracks as he rounded the corner.

"Can I help you?" a middle aged blonde asked.

"Vicki Lewis?"

The woman's eyes widened. "Do I know you?"

Riley shook his head. "I'm sorry. But . . . you're here?"

She took a step back, fear written in her gaze. "Do I need to call the police?"

"I'm sorry. I'm not trying to scare you. But someone said you were missing. They thought you might even be dead. But here you are."

A women's shelter ran this place. That was right. What if . . . ?

"I'm just staying here until I can get back on my feet. I took some leave from work because I was afraid my ex would track me down."

"I'm sorry to hear that. I didn't mean to overstep. I just saw Mr. Parksley pull away and . . ." He shook his head.

"He knows I'm here. He and his wife have been good friends. He dropped some money by for me to help me get back on my feet."

"He's helping you?"

She nodded. "Of course he is. He was the best boss I ever had. I hated to see him go."

"I guess he got out right in time, huh? Right before this scandal broke out at the hospital?"

She shrugged. "It's going to be a headache, for sure. He was the one who reported it initially."

"Are you sure?"

She nodded. "Positive. Now, if you'll excuse me, I have to get back to work."

Riley mulled over what he'd learned as he walked back

toward the front of the building. On a whim, he slipped inside the store. His thoughts were beginning to crush him, to make him feel defeated. But while he was here, he decided to check on one more thing.

When he walked in, someone other than Shirley was working at the front desk. This woman was in her mid-twenties with light brown hair pulled back into a tight ponytail. She wore a flannel shirt and still had a smattering of acne.

Could this be Robin?

"Can I help you?" she asked, shoving aside a magazine as Riley approached.

"I hope so. I'm looking for a rug. I think it was donated a couple of weeks ago."

"A rug? What kind?"

"An area rug. Beige and burgundy."

"Very specific." She nodded almost comically.

He shrugged. "Someone I know dropped it off for donation before they knew I wanted it."

She frowned, an unexpected reaction. "Someone did drop off a rug. Mr. Parksley."

Riley's eyes widened. "He's the one. You know him?"

She nodded. "I do. We talked quite a bit, actually. He donated a rug and some shoes. I actually bought the rug myself, though."

"What?" This couldn't be right?

She nodded again. "It looked practically new. I couldn't pass it up. We didn't even put it out on the floor."

Riley shook his head, not willing to accept the heavy realizations that felt like they could sink him. "When did he do this?"

She shrugged. "I can't say for sure. It was one weekend not long ago, though. Maybe a couple of weeks?"

"And the rug looked new?"

"That's right." She pulled out her phone. "I even took a picture of it in my apartment. Here it is."

Sure enough, it looked like the same rug. Riley shook his head and squeezed the skin between his eyes.

"Is everything okay?"

Riley stepped back, his head swimming. "Yeah, it's fine. Thanks for your help."

He left the thrift store, hardly able to breathe.

Because he had a terrible realization.

He really was losing his mind.

CHAPTER 20

How could he have been so wrong? All along, that sound he'd heard must have been a car backfiring. Mr. Parksley had taken some items to the thrift store. The blood Riley thought he saw . . . that must have been some type of flashback.

Maybe everyone had been right all along. Riley wasn't ready to be on his own. He wasn't ready to regain any independence. And he needed to face the fact that he might not ever be ready. His life was forever changed.

Two days after his visit to the thrift store, Riley almost felt depressed and he was spending way too much time up in his room, thinking too much and not praying enough. Which was what he did now. The shades were drawn, everything silent around him.

As he mentally replayed the events of the past couple of weeks, someone knocked at his door and pulled him from his thoughts. Who could that be? His parents had both gone out to meet with their financial planner about this year's taxes.

"Come in," he muttered.

Sophia walked in. "You're going to the dojo with me."

"I don't feel like it."

She pursed her lips in a scowl. "Wrong answer. You're going. Just because you were wrong about one thing doesn't mean you should shut down."

"I was apparently wrong about quite a bit."

"There's something I want to tell you. But you have to go to Todd's with me first."

What could she possibly have to tell him? "I don't know."

"Come on, Riley. Get out of the house. You're not doing yourself any favors sitting around and feeling sorry for yourself."

"I'm not feeling sorry for myself."

"Could have fooled me. Prove yourself by coming with me."

Begrudgingly, he met her downstairs ten minutes later and they went to the dojo. He had to admit that the workout felt good. But it still didn't break the melancholy that shrouded him.

After their session ended, Todd suggested they all grab dinner together. Sophia quickly agreed, so they headed to a Southern-Italian restaurant. Riley had little choice but to go along since Sophia was his ride.

"So, I think you'll find this really interesting, Riley," Sophia started, taking a sip of iced tea. "Dr. Perkins just announced that she's writing a book."

Riley waited, not sure what was so interesting about that. "Okay . . .?"

"It's about relationships after traumatic brain injury," Sophia finished.

"Not to be a broken record, but okay . . ."

She nodded. "Apparently, the whole premise of the book is that relationships never work. She has case study after case study to prove it."

"As interesting as that is, what does it have to do with me?"

She sucked in a long breath. "It's like this. Studies are supposed to be objective. You're supposed to go in with an open mind. But Dr. Perkins, rumor has it, isn't like that. She came in with a theory that she wanted to prove and she didn't back down."

Riley shifted in his seat, suddenly interested. "Are you saying what I think you're saying?"

"I am if you think I'm saying that all of the advice that she's given you has been through the filter of this book."

Riley straightened some. "So, all of that talk about having no hope for success could have been wrong?"

Sophia shrugged. "I'm not saying there's no merit to the studies or the statistics, but I am saying that I really feel she was pushing her own agenda. When someone plants an idea in a person's mind that a relationship won't work, sometimes the very suggestion can shape the future. If she did, then the results would only help to prove her theory."

"Is that even ethical?" Riley asked.

"Not really. Will anyone call her out on it? It's hard to say. It's hard to prove intent. I just thought you'd want to know."

"Surprisingly, that does make me feel a little better." One of the main reasons he'd decided not to go back to her anymore was because she didn't share the same biblical foundations. Riley believed that with reliance on God's word and prayer that anything could happen. Dr. Perkins had led him to believe otherwise. But his relationships were about more than circumstances and external measures. They were also about faith and commitment. Somewhere along the line, he'd started to believe what Dr. Perkins told him was the truth. He was so glad he'd decided not to go back to her. He needed to meet with someone who shared his worldview.

"Everything okay?" Todd asked as their food came out. The waitress set a huge salad in front of him. Riley had ordered fried chicken marsala, and Sophia got chicken and angel hair dumplings.

"Rough week," Riley muttered.

"I was just reading this morning about how our trials are

temporary," Todd said. "I know they may not feel like it. But everything will pass in time."

Riley nodded half-heartedly. "Thanks."

He didn't say anything else, so Todd and Sophia eventually got the hint that he didn't want to talk.

"So, what's all of this stress you keep talking about?" Todd asked Sophia. "You look tense today."

His cousin had been especially aggressive on the punching bag earlier, making it obvious she had a lot of pent up frustration inside. Something about the way Todd said the words made Riley wonder if the two of them had talked outside of the dojo recently, though.

Sophia let out a sigh and took a long sip of her tea. "It's all of the craziness at the hospital right now."

"Yeah, what's going on?" Todd asked. "I saw something on the news."

"Someone on staff has been stealing drugs. Even worse, they think that my supervisor who's been gone didn't just go on vacation. They think that she skipped town."

"Sounds like a mess," Todd said.

"Tell me about it. The authorities are all over the place. They're trying to track down Gretchen on vacation, but she won't answer her phone. She's probably out shopping for new Jimmy Choos."

Riley suddenly straightened. "What did you say?"

"That they're trying to track down Gretchen—"

"No, after that. Something about shoes?"

Sophia shrugged. "Gretchen loved Jimmy Choos. Why?"

"She didn't wear a size eleven, did she?"

Sophia went still. "She always complained because she thought she had big feet. Why are you asking?"

Riley shook his head, trying to sort everything out. It

couldn't be . . . could it? But the brand of shoe and the size couldn't be a coincidence.

Or could it?

Nothing seemed certain anymore.

"Riley, what are you thinking about?" Sophia asked.

"You'll think I'm crazy."

"Try me."

He pulled out his phone and showed Sophia the picture he'd taken that day at Mr. Parksley's. "Does this look familiar?"

"Yeah, it's the shoe you found that day you thought you heard the gunshot."

"Look closer."

She studied it a moment before her eyes widened. "Size eleven Jimmy Choos. It could be a coincidence."

"You said no one has heard from Gretchen in how long?"

Sophia swallowed hard. "It's been a while. A . . . couple of weeks, at least."

Riley stared at her.

She finally shook her head. "I don't know, Riley."

"What's going on?" Todd asked.

Sophia and Riley stared at each other a moment before finally Riley spoke. "I thought I heard my neighbor shoot someone and then saw him try and cover it up. No one believes me. I'm not sure I believe me half of the time."

"Whoa. That's . . . heavy."

Riley nodded. "I know. But I've had absolutely no proof. All I have is a brain that isn't working correctly. I have no body, no idea whose body it might be, no weapon. Nothing."

"Until now," Todd said.

Riley shook his head, remembering the letdown of discovering the donated rug. "And again, I have no way to prove anything. Just an idea. If I keep pursuing this, my parents are going to put me in the looney bin."

"Maybe we can put your mind at rest. What if Sophia and I help you?" He glanced at Sophia. "If that's okay with you."

She shrugged. "Sure, I guess."

"What motive would Mr. Parksley have for murdering this woman? Does he even know her?" Todd asked.

Riley nodded. "They would have both worked at the hospital."

"And the drugs have been going missing, and the fact that someone has been ordering supplies and padding the invoices," Sophia said. "They've been splitting the differences with the provider. Mr. Parksley could have been involved."

Riley nodded. "That's right. He was the CFO. He had a front row seat to all of that financial information. If anyone could get away with it, it would have been Mr. Parksley."

Sophia went pale. "He would have been working at the hospital when all of it happened."

"How about Gretchen? Was she working there at the time?" Todd asked.

Sophia nodded. "She was there. She's probably been at the hospital for five years."

"Is there a chance she could have known something that would incriminate Mr. Parksley?" Todd asked.

Riley nodded, a new idea hitting him. "It's a theory. He could have killed her and then dumped her body into the lake behind his property."

"Dumped her body into the lake . . . what?" Sophia asked, shaking her head.

"It's just a theory. I can't exactly go scuba diving in the lake to see if it's true, nor can I tell the police without any evidence to back it up. But it's all starting to make sense."

"Let's say that's true. What do we do?" Todd asked.

Riley appreciated the "we" in his sentence, especially since he wasn't completely trusting himself at this very moment.

"How about we go for a boat ride?" Riley asked.

CHAPTER 21

Thirty minutes later, Todd, Sophia, and Riley were all in an old canoe gliding across the water. Riley's parents had looked at them like they were crazy when they heard what they were doing. But since Sophia and Todd were there, they probably just thought they were reliving their goofy teenage years and didn't ask too many questions.

It was cold outside—too cold to be out on the water. But they all wore hats and scarves and coats. The day was gray and winter-like and seemed a good reflection of the dreary implications this investigation could have.

"What exactly are we hoping to discover?" Sophia asked.

Riley shrugged. "I have no idea. It's all kind of vague. But I just need some type of proof. Maybe having a different perspective will help me to see something I haven't seen before."

Todd and Riley did most of the rowing. Something about being out in the cold air and doing something risky invigorated Riley. Life had just been a series of routines, of struggling to get by day by day for so long. It felt good to be excited.

In fact, for the past couple of weeks—give or take a few days—he'd felt more alive than he had in a long time. Though he'd still struggled, he'd had something to think about other than all the things that were wrong in his life. Dwelling on this unofficial investigation had been a nice distraction.

"That's his house?" Sophia asked, nodding toward the

shore.

Riley nodded. "That's the one."

"Nice place," Todd said. "I could probably put ten of my apartments in that square footage."

When Riley thought of the times that he'd been in Mr. Parksley's house as the man had taught him to whittle, a bittersweet feeling filled him. He'd actually had moments when he had enjoyed himself. If he found evidence that proved Mr. Parksley had killed someone, Mr. Parksley would be going away for a long time. It seemed a shame that someone would throw away his life like that.

They finally crept around to the other side of a small peninsula of trees.

"Mr. Parksley owns all of this land. It would be the perfect place to dump evidence." *Or a body.* Riley couldn't bring himself to say the last part, though.

"You and Todd already checked out the woods?" Sophia asked.

"Only part of the woods," Todd said. "It would take hours to search the entire area, plus we'd be trespassing."

They rowed closer to the land and paused, staring at the shoreline a moment.

"So, what if Mr. Parksley killed Gretchen, let's say. Maybe he pulled his truck up to the water, weighed her down, and dumped her here," Riley said.

"But what did he weigh her down with? Did he just happen to have something on hand?" Sophia asked.

"I have no idea. A spare tire? An old toolbox?" Riley was trying to think of things that would have been in Mr. Parksley's truck. "The other thing that bothers me is how did she get to his house? There were no other cars there."

"What if she parked somewhere else?" Todd asked.

"Why would she do that?" Sophia asked, her breath frosty in front of her face.

"Maybe they had a secret meeting," Todd suggested. "Maybe she went there, hoping her car wouldn't be seen, so she stashed it somewhere else."

"But why would she do that?" Sophia asked again.

"Because she had something to hide," Riley said.

"You're not suggesting an affair, are you?" Her eyes widened. "Although, she always had expensive clothes and even drove a car that seemed far beyond her income. I don't claim to know any of the details of her life. Maybe her parents are rich. But I always thought it was odd that someone like her could afford the things she afforded."

"So you think Mr. Parksley bought those things for her? Maybe as a way of keeping her quiet?" Todd asked.

She shrugged. "It's just a theory—and there are no bad ideas when you're brainstorming."

"I think it's a pretty good idea," Todd said.

Riley looked away and tried not to roll his eyes. Those two just needed to admit their feelings for each other and start dating.

"Unfortunately, ideas aren't going to get us very far. We need proof." Riley felt like a killjoy as soon as he said the words. "So maybe we can find some tire tracks or something?"

"That's a good idea," Todd said. "We'll row along the shoreline. There are only a few places that a truck could fit back here. We should be able to rule a lot of this out."

As they glided along the water, Riley searched for something that would connect dots in his head. This could all be for nothing, but he really hoped it wasn't.

"Check that out over there!" Riley pointed to a small stretch of shoreline in the distance.

They rowed that way, pausing as they got closer.

"It looks like some kind of service road," Todd said.

Riley pointed to an old fishing boat. "Or maybe an access road for fishermen."

The canoe hit the shore and wobbled for a moment. Carefully, Riley stood and stepped onto the damp soil by the water.

As soon as his feet hit the ground, something caught his eye. "Look, those are tire tracks. It's weird. These tracks almost look like they go right into the water."

Todd helped Sophia out before pulling the canoe farther onto the shore. They all examined the tracks for a moment, but the evidence was solidifying in Riley's mind. The lake, at its deepest, was probably 14 feet. That was plenty of depth to conceal a body.

On a hunch, he began to follow the tire tracks. The trees were just far enough apart for a car or truck to squeeze through. He wasn't sure where the access to this area was, but someone obviously knew. Most likely, the person who owned this property.

He stopped midway into the woods and stared at the ground again. He squatted to get a better look. "This is strange. These are two different sets of tires. Look at the tread. They're not the same."

Todd bent down beside him, his jaw set in a hard line. "You're right. There have been two vehicles here recently. But why two?"

"Because Gretchen parked here," Riley realized. "Mr. Parksley drove back here with her body, put her into the car, and then pushed it into the water. It was the perfect location because that stretch of trees would conceal it from anyone around."

Sophia glanced toward the distance, her eyes widening. "You guys, I think I hear something. Is that a car coming down the road?"

"The road's too far away," Riley said, shaking his head. "That car's coming through the woods."

They ducked into the woods just as a truck appeared in the distance. Staying concealed behind a cluster of trees, Riley peeked out, being sure to stay low so he wouldn't be spotted.

As soon as he had a better view of the vehicle, Riley knew exactly whom it belonged to.

Mr. Parksley.

CHAPTER 22

Riley watched motionlessly as Mr. Parksley pulled near the lake, parked his truck, and stepped outside. The man stuffed his hands into the pockets of his leather jacket and stood looking over the lake silently.

What was he doing? Reflecting on what he'd gotten away with? Smirking because he thought he was more clever than the police?

At once, Riley pictured the man coming out here each day, reflecting on his devious acts. How could someone who seemed so kind be capable of this? How could he live with himself?

Just then, a twig cracked behind them. Riley jerked his head toward the sound and saw Sophia's mouth drop open. "I'm sorry," she mouthed.

Riley swung his head back toward the lake. Mr. Parksley's gaze shot their way. He'd heard it also.

"Who's there?" Mr. Parksley called, peering into the woods.

Riley and Todd exchanged a look. It was only a matter of time before they were discovered. Certainly they could outrun the man. But Riley had a different idea. He was tired of the fear, of regret.

"Stay there with Sophia," Riley whispered to Todd. "And call the police."

"You sure about this?" Todd asked, gripping Riley's shoulder.

Riley nodded, not really sure about anything. But it was

time to put an end to all of this speculation. If Riley was correct and Mr. Parksley was a killer, then the police needed to know. He only hoped they arrived before Mr. Parksley took drastic measures.

Riley stepped out and stiffly walked toward the shoreline. "It's me, Mr. Parksley."

"Riley?" Surprise registered on his face. "What are you doing out here?"

He nodded toward the canoe in the distance, which was only partially concealed by marsh grass. "Took a little boat ride earlier. Then I heard someone coming and got nervous."

"You know this is private property, right?" One hand remained in Mr. Parksley's pocket. Did he have a gun in there? Riley couldn't be sure, but he needed to remain on guard, just in case.

Riley nodded. "I do realize that."

"I don't mind if you use it. Just ask me first. I let my friends who fish come out here all the time."

Riley swallowed hard, wanting to choose his words carefully. "Mr. Parksley, I heard about what's going on at the hospital, with the missing drugs."

The man straightened, his entire body looking rigid and uptight. "I'm well aware of the situation."

"That had to be stressful for you as CFO. You probably knew about it months ago."

"It's an ongoing investigation. I can't comment." The wrinkles on his face seemed to deepen as he frowned.

"What about Gretchen?" Riley asked. It was a risky move, but he still had no evidence. Maybe confrontation wasn't the best idea. However, he knew he had no other choice but to have this conversation.

Mr. Parksley's eyes widened. "Gretchen?"

"The nurse. She's the one you shot, isn't she?"

The man's skin went pale and he took a step back. "What are you talking about?"

"I was taking a walk behind your house that day when I heard the gunshot. I'm the one who called the police. Fortunately for you, you had everything cleaned up before the detective got to your house that evening."

Mr. Parksley's hand remained in his pocket, and Riley had to wonder about what was concealed there. In his mind, Riley could still feel the gunshot wound, he could still feel the repercussions the crime had on his life. Flashbacks began to hound him, begging for his attention, begging for . . . his entire life? That's what his injury had become, wasn't it? Something that defined his existence.

He needed to change that.

"I don't know what you're talking about," Mr. Parksley said with a weak laugh. "Are you sure your medications are what they should be?"

"I saw the shoe outside by your truck after you dragged the rug outside. It was a size 11 Jimmy Choo. Gretchen just happened to have an affinity for Jimmy Choos and was always lamenting about the size of her feet." It was his ace card, the one sure fact that proved something had happened.

Mr. Parksley's skin looked even paler than usual. "Why would I kill anyone? The idea is . . . crazy. If you keep talking like this, I'm going to have to call the police."

"You told me you didn't own a gun. But you do. You hunt."

"I got rid of my guns years ago after some pressure from my wife. She doesn't believe in guns."

"That doesn't mean you don't have a gun or that you couldn't get one from a friend."

Something changed in Mr. Parksley eyes. The denial faded.

But a new emotion rose to the surface. Could it be . . . regret? No. That couldn't be it. Anger and rage made more sense.

"I knew you were the one who called the police, Riley." Mr. Parksley continued to stare at him. "You're the only person who takes walks around the lake. It's just one of the reasons I volunteered to teach you to whittle. I wanted to keep an eye on you as well. You have to admit: that's the only reason you agreed to take lessons. You wanted to keep an eye on me also. But things aren't always as they seem, Riley."

Riley shook his head, unable to comprehend where the man was going with this. "What do you mean?"

Mr. Parksley's hand came out of his pocket, and Riley braced himself to see the gun, to hear it fire, to feel the intense pain that followed.

Riley raised his hand, urging his neighbor to stop. "Mr. Parksley, my friends just called the police. I wouldn't do anything rash now. You'll only regret it."

Mr. Parksley held up his cell phone. No gun. Thank God it wasn't a gun. Riley's heart rate slowed, but only slightly.

"I knew exactly what everyone would think," his neighbor continued. "That's why I saved all of the text messages between Gretchen and myself."

Riley remembered the other theory that had been thrown out there. Sophia had said Gretchen had a lot of money. Was that because of Mr. Parksley and some kind of off-limits relationship? "So you really were having an affair?"

"An affair? Certainly not. I'm a married man! You've got this all wrong." His gaze flicked behind Riley and he took a step back. "I see you brought backup."

Todd and Sophia stepped out from the brush. Now that they knew the man didn't have a gun, they must have figured the coast was clear. It was a pretty safe bet.

"Sophia?" Mr. Parksley asked.

"Hello, Mr. Parksley." She nodded and clasped her hands in front of her as if the confrontation made her uncomfortable.

"An affair is the only thing that makes sense," Riley continued. "She must have parked down here so no one would see her car. You drove your truck back here, with her body wrapped up in that rug. My guess is that you put the body into her car and then pushed both of them into this lake. It's the only thing that fits."

He shook his head, pinching the skin between his eyes. "I knew it was only a matter of time before someone figured it out. I'm surprised I got away with it for as long as I did."

"How could you take someone's life?" Sophia questioned. "I . . . I looked up to you."

Mr. Parksley shook his head again. "That's where you have it wrong. I didn't kill Gretchen."

"Then what happened?" Riley asked, fighting desperately to keep his thoughts under control.

Mr. Parksley's shoulders drooped. "You have a lot of the story right. Gretchen did park here, and she snuck to my house to meet with me. But she was trying to convince me to get rid of all of the evidence that she was guilty."

"Guilty?" Riley repeated.

Mr. Parksley nodded, his voice listless. "That's right. She was the one stealing drugs from the hospital. How else do you think she afforded her lifestyle?"

Sophia gasped. "Gretchen really was behind the drugs? I kept hoping that everyone was wrong and she was above all of that."

Mr. Parksley nodded again. "I'd had suspicions for a while. I confronted Gretchen, and she tried to tell me I was wrong. I found the proof I needed to take to the authorities. Gretchen came to my house to convince me not to."

"So you killed her?" Riley asked. "Were you trying to save your reputation? Was she trying to incriminate you in some way?"

He shook his head. "No, *she* pulled out a gun on *me*. She was crazy. I think all the stress finally caught up with her and she was desperate. She was going to kill me before I took the information public."

"What?" Riley's hands went to his hips as his thoughts collided.

"It's true. She pulled the gun out, and I knew she was unhinged enough to pull the trigger. We struggled. The gun fired. The bullet hit her in the chest, and she died almost immediately." He let out a soft moan.

"So why didn't you call the police?" Riley asked.

Mr. Parksley's head swung back in forth with agony. "I panicked. I didn't know what to do. So I wrapped her in my rug and dragged her out to my truck. Everything else happened as you said."

"So you did dump her here?" Riley clarified.

"I did. As soon as I got back home, I scrubbed everything down. After the police came and talked to me, I went out and bought another rug. I scuffed it up a little bit, and then donated it, along with some old shoes, just in case anyone got suspicious. But this whole thing has been haunting me ever since."

"Is that why you're here now?" Sophia asked, a touch of compassion replacing her outrage.

Mr. Parksley nodded. "It is. I can't get over my guilt. I may not have killed her, but I didn't do right by her either. And now I've gotten myself in a world of trouble."

"Why didn't you just come forward?" Todd asked.

"I kept justifying it to myself. You see, my wife isn't at a spa. She's in rehab. She's an alcoholic. And that jewelry that went missing? The maid didn't take it. My wife just called last night and owned up to the fact that she hocked it in order to have more money to fund her habits."

"It sounds like she has a lot of problems," Riley said.

"I feared if news got out about what happened that she'd turn back to the bottle again, that all of her recovery would be for nothing. Then so much time had passed that I knew how it would look either way."

"The police might be lenient on you when you tell them what happened," Todd said, standing tall and strong, just like a good soldier might. "You'll probably get involuntary manslaughter, at the most. Obstruction of justice, at the least."

Just then, sirens wailed in the distance. Two police cars pulled up, and Detective Gray stepped out.

Mr. Parksley nodded in resignation. "I need to tell you something, Detective Gray."

CHAPTER 23

That night, after the police had taken statements, everyone gathered in Riley's parents' home. His mom fixed some gingerbread cookies and hot chocolate, and they all gathered in the living room to explain what had happened. For the first time in a long time, Riley felt like celebrating.

Except he didn't.

He hated to think of the consequences of Mr. Parksley's actions. He only wished the man had called the police right away. Todd's words were probably correct, though. He doubted Mr. Parksley would do any time in prison. Maybe he'd get some community service and a fine. It was hard to say.

"I'm sorry we doubted you, Son," Riley's dad said, placing his heavy hand on his shoulder.

"I know it was a crazy story," Riley conceded. "I would have probably doubted my story also if I hadn't lived it."

"Maybe you can finally put your mind at ease." He shifted. "My friend wants to talk to you, by the way. Jim Gleason was impressed with your previous work with the law firm, and his firm is wanting to hire someone to take over social justice cases."

"I really don't want to do anything permanent right now, especially not in this area. You know I want to go back to Norfolk."

"Just hear him out. There's a lot of flexibility in it. And

stability. I really think it could work for you. As soon as the doctor approves your clearance, of course."

"I'm not making any promises. But I'll talk to him." Riley had no desire to settle down in this area. But he did need to get his foot in the door again. He would keep his options open. If he didn't have an income, there was no way he could move out on his own again.

He had to remind himself to take baby steps forward.

"Thank you," his father conceded.

Sophia, who'd been having her own private conversation with Todd on the couch since they arrived, finally stood. "I'm going to get going. It's been a long day."

Todd stood beside her. "Same here. I'm . . . uh, I'm going to drive Sophia . . . back to her car. Better yet, how about if we get some dinner to celebrate?"

"Yeah, that sounds great." Her grin slipped. "You want to join us, Riley?"

Riley shook his head. "No, I think I'll let you two go enjoy yourselves. I could use some rest anyway."

As Todd and Sophia exchanged a secretive smile, Riley's heart panged with sorrow. While he was happy for the two of them, seeing them together made him realize what he'd lost.

A few minutes later, as he headed to his room, he reflected about poor decisions made under distress.

Gretchen had taken a gun to Mr. Parksley's house in desperation to save herself.

Mr. Parksley had hidden Gretchen's body out of fear he'd look bad. In the process, he'd only made himself look worse.

Riley had also made some bad choices in the heat of the moment. Breaking up with Gabby was one of the biggest. He wished he'd listened to his own gut instead of listening to everyone else.

How would he win her back?

He shook his head, wishing he had a magical solution. But he didn't. *What should I do, Lord?*

The same urging he'd felt present in his life remained.

Wait.

He looked up at the ceiling. *Really, God?*

In his heart, he knew the answer. He needed to wait. He still had some things to work through before he could move back.

When the time was right, he would tell Gabby everything, though. And he prayed that what Pastor Randy had told him would be true: That God could take our mistakes and turn them into testimonies that would help others. He'd take our messes and turn them into messages.

God did have a plan, even for Riley's ordeal. Riley just had to wait on God's timing, God's prompting, God's wisdom. Because, when everything else was stripped away, faith was all a person had to hang onto.

###

Look for these books in the Squeaky Clean series:

Hazardous Duty (Book 1)

On her way to completing a degree in forensic science, Gabby St. Claire drops out of school and starts her own crime scene cleaning business. "Yeah, that's me," she says, "a crime scene cleaner. People waiting in line behind me who strike up conversations always regret it."

When a routine cleaning job uncovers a murder weapon the police overlooked, she realizes that the wrong person is in jail. But the owner of the weapon is a powerful foe . . . and willing to do anything to keep Gabby quiet.

With the help of her new neighbor, Riley Thomas, a man whose life and faith fascinate her, Gabby plays the detective to make sure the right person is put behind bars. Can Riley help her before another murder occurs?

Suspicious Minds (Book 2)

In this smart and suspenseful sequel to *Hazardous Duty*, crime scene cleaner Gabby St. Claire finds herself stuck doing mold remediation to pay the bills. But her first day on the job, she uncovers a surprise in the crawlspace of a dilapidated home: Elvis, dead as a doornail and still wearing his blue suede shoes. How could she possibly keep her nose out of a case like this?

It Came Upon a Midnight Crime (Book 2.5, a Novella)

Someone is intent on destroying the true meaning of Christmas—at least, destroying anything that hints of it. All around crime scene cleaner Gabby St. Claire's hometown, anything pointing to Jesus as the "reason for the season" is being sabotaged. The crimes become more twisted as dismembered body parts are found at the vandalisms. Who would go to such great lengths to dampen the joy and hope of Christ's birthday? Someone's determined to destroy Christmas . . . but Gabby St. Claire is just as determined to find the Grinch and let peace on earth and goodwill to men prevail.

Organized Grime (Book 3)
Gabby St. Claire knows her best friend, Sierra, isn't guilty of killing three people in what appears to be an eco-terrorist attack. But Sierra has disappeared, her only contact a frantic phone call to Gabby proclaiming that she's being hunted. Gabby is determined to prove her friend is innocent and to keep her alive. While trying to track down the real perpetrator, Gabby notices a disturbing trend at the crime scenes she's cleaning, one that ties random crimes together—and points to Sierra as the guilty party. Just what has her friend gotten herself into?

Dirty Deeds (Book 4)
"Promise me one thing. No snooping. Just for one week."

Gabby St. Claire knows that her fiancé's request is a simple one that she should be able to honor. After all, Riley's law school reunion and attorneys' conference at a hoity-toity resort is a chance for them to get away from the mysteries Gabby often finds herself involved in as a crime scene cleaner. The weeklong trip is a chance for them to be "normal," a word that leaves a bad taste in Gabby's mouth.

But Gabby finds herself alone for endless hours while Riley is

WHILE YOU WERE SWEEPING

busy with legal workshops. Then one of Riley's old friends goes missing, and Gabby suspects one of Riley's buddies might be behind the disappearance. When the missing woman's mom asks Gabby for help, how can she say no?

Secrets abound. Frankly, Gabby even has some of her own. When the dirty truth comes out, the revelations put everything in jeopardy—relationships, trusts, and even lives.

The Scum of All Fears (Book 5)
"I'll get out, and I'll get even."

Gabby St. Claire is back to crime-scene cleaning, at least temporarily. With her business partner on his honeymoon, she needs help after a weekend killing spree fills up her work docket. She quickly realizes she has bigger problems than finding temporary help.

A serial killer her fiancé, a former prosecutor, put behind bars has escaped. His last words to Riley were: *I'll get out, and I'll get even.* Pictures of Gabby are found in the man's prison cell, and Riley fears the sadistic madman has Gabby in his sights.

Gabby tells herself there's no way the Scum River Killer will make it across the country from California to Virginia without being caught. But then messages are left for Gabby at crime scenes, and someone keeps slipping in and out of her apartment.

When Gabby's temporary assistant disappears, Gabby must figure out who's behind these crimes. The search for answers becomes darker when Gabby realizes she's dealing with a criminal who's more than evil. He's truly the scum of the earth, and he'll do anything to make Gabby and Riley's lives a living nightmare.

To Love, Honor, and Perish (Book 6)

How could God let this happen?

Crime scene cleaner Gabby St. Claire can't stop asking the question. Just when her life is on the right track, the unthinkable happens. Gabby's fiancé, Riley Thomas, is shot and remains in life-threatening condition only a week before their wedding.

Gabby is determined to figure out who pulled the trigger, even if investigating puts her own life at risk. But as she digs deeper into the facts surrounding the case, she discovers secrets better left alone. Doubts arise in her mind and the one man with answers is on death's doorstep.

An old foe from the past returns and tests everything Gabby is made of—physically, mentally, and spiritually. Will her soul survive the challenges ahead? Or will everything she's worked for be destroyed?

Mucky Streak (Book 7)

After her last encounter with a serial killer, Gabby St. Claire feels her life is smeared with the stain of tragedy. Between the exhaustion of trying to get her fiancé back on his feet, routine night terrors, and potential changes looming on the horizon, she needs a respite from the mire of life.

At the encouragement of her friends, she takes on a short-term gig as a private investigator: a cold case that's eluded investigators for ten years. The mass murder of a wealthy family seems impossible to solve but quickly gets interesting as Gabby brings more clues to light. Add to the mix a flirtatious client, travels to an exciting new city, and some quirky—albeit temporary—new sidekicks, and things get really complicated.

With every new development, Gabby prays that what she's calling her "mucky streak" will end and the future will become clear. But every answer she uncovers leads her closer to danger—both for her life and for her heart.

Foul Play (Book 8)
Gabby St. Claire is crying foul play, in every sense of the phrase.

When crime scene cleaner Gabby St. Claire agrees to go undercover at a local community theater, she discovers more than backstage bickering, atrocious acting, and rotten writing. The female lead is dead and an old classmate who's staked everything on the musical production's success is about to go under.

In her dual role of investigator and star of the show, Gabby finds the stakes rising faster than the opening night curtain. She comes face to face with her past and must make monumental decisions, not just about the play but also concerning her future relationships and career.

Will Gabby find the killer before the curtain goes down—not only on the play, but also on life as she knows it?

Coming Soon:
Dust and Obey (Book 10)

About the Author:

USA Today has called Christy Barritt's books "scary, funny, passionate, and quirky."
Christy writes both mystery and romantic suspense novels that are clean with underlying messages of faith. Her books have won the Daphne du Maurier Award for Excellence in Suspense and Mystery, have been twice nominated for the Romantic Times' Reviewers' Choice Award, and have finaled for both a Carol Award and Foreword Magazine's Book of the Year.

She's married to her Prince Charming, a man who thinks she's hilarious--but only when she's not trying to be. Christy's a self-proclaimed klutz, an avid music lover who's known for spontaneously bursting into song, and a road trip aficionado.

When she's not working or spending time with her family, she enjoys singing, playing the guitar, and exploring small, unsuspecting towns where people have no idea how accident prone she is.

Find Christy online at:
www.christybarritt.com
www.facebook.com/christybarritt
www.twitter.com/cbarritt

Sign up for Christy's newsletter to get information on all of her latest releases here: www.christybarritt.com/newsletter-sign-up/

If you enjoyed this book, please consider leaving a review.

42910659R00079

Made in the USA
Middletown, DE
24 April 2017